THE TURN OF THE SCREW

THE LESSON OF
THE MASTER

THE TURN
OF THE SCREW

◆

THE LESSON OF
THE MASTER

◆

By Henry James

Introduction by HEYWOOD BROUN

THE
MODERN LIBRARY
NEW YORK

Random House IS THE PUBLISHER OF

THE MODERN LIBRARY

BENNETT A. CERF · DONALD S. KLOPFER · ROBERT K. HAAS

Manufactured in the United States of America

By H. Wolff

INTRODUCTION

I CAME across "The Turn of the Screw" by accident, though goodness knows I had heard enough of it by name. Even in those early days it was known to me by reputation as the thriller of thrillers, the last word in creeping horror stories. But I am by natural bent a timid man, and can get all I want of terror by the contemplation of my own life and its circumstances, without reaching out for those not normally on my own horizon. I knew very well that Mr. James must have done a superb job, because all the friends I had for whose opinion I had any affection had assured me that he had, and moreover I knew a little something about Mr. James. He was not to be sneezed at, no matter what he set himself to do. But though time after time I had been admonished to read "The Turn of the Screw," and time after time I had said graciously I certainly would, I had no earthly intention of doing it. Not for me, I said, these vicarious chills and fever.

But there did come a man who said, one day, "Have you ever read a story by Henry James called 'The Beast in the Jungle'?" and, upon my admission that I never had, he read me such a lecture as I have seldom heard. It was, he said, one of the few great short stories in the English language, and not to have read it was to go wantonly through life minus a definitely great experience.

Well, we talked about "The Beast in the Jungle," and I learned that it was in a collection of James stories called "The Better Sort."

I was living at the time in the Swiss Alps, in a small wooden chalet which gave on the Dents du Midi and the Rhone Valley, with windows disproportionately large for a country which had in part the fact and in part the echo of a window tax, where you could look over thirty or forty miles of crystalline nothingness the moment you opened your eyes in the morning, and where you could not have escaped the sense of being on an eagle's perch if you had been stupid enough to try. The chalet's windows—and its doors too—opened onto the Rhone Valley. If you sat in the middle of the floor, you could see nothing but sky and snow covered peaks. Even if you went to a door or window, the natural drop of the land was such that you had to peer downwards quite considerably to find earth fellow to that on which your house was built.

At the time of which I speak, and in the circumstances, the way of living was at once free and circumscribed. It was possible to get all manner of luxuries, if you could pay for them, by way of the parcels post. Some of you may remember that before the war, the Swiss and the Germans were using the parcels post as competently as we came to use it later here, and that you could do well by yourself in the farthest hamlet if you knew where to send your orders. For example, it was possible to smoke the most admirable cigarettes in this woodsmen's village where I lived, and where my fellow townsmen made shift with true tobacconistic horrors for want of proper enterprise, by knowing just how to send for a really good cigarette. It was also possible, in theory at any rate, to order one's books. You may remember that those were the days of the Tauchnitz editions, and that for forty cents we could get H. G. Wells' "Passionate Friends," Galsworthy's "The Dark Flower," any amount of good Anne Douglas Sedgewick, Norman Douglas, and so on.

Well, it was, again in theory, possible to get Henry James, except that one had to write to London for him, since he was not current, and therefore not in Tauchnitz. The procedure for getting James was to run down to

Montreux, get either a Paris edition of the New York *Herald* or a Paris and London *Daily Mail* and find out the London addresses of the leading London bookshops. Armed with three of these, and prodded by my Jamesian friend who would have me read "The Beast in the Jungle," if my eyes dropped out, I sent off postcards to have "The Better Sort" sent to me as soon as possible. One bookshop replied that Mr. James had never written a book of that title, another that it was then in process of being published—it had been out some five or six years —and the third that Mr. Henry James had written only one distinguished short story, "The Turn of the Screw," that I must surely have made a mistake in the title, and that "The Turn of the Screw" was being sent to me under separate cover.

Well, there I was, of course, in my lonely roost in the high Alps, with "The Turn of the Screw" on its way to me, and no way of stopping it since parcels post debts were in those days in a class with poker debts as a call on one's honor. And only the companionship of the frosted hill tops to keep me from being frightened right out of my wits.

For two or three days after it came, I would not even open the parcel. I knew perfectly well what was going to happen to me—that I would wake up staring in the darkness of the night, seeing the baleful eyes of the butler at my window, watching the cowering figures of children in the shadowy corners of my room, bound helplessly in the spell of this man James whose piratical hold over other men's imaginations I could do nothing whatever against.

I did finally bring myself to the scratch. I opened the book, read a little of it, and then a little more, and, of course, finished it in precisely that hideous thralldom that had been its author's wicked purpose. And there was no clammy sensation I did not sense. There was no sinister horror I did not live through. For nights and nights I would no more than cajole myself to sleep than I would wake staring out of my windows, glazed eyes fixed on the icy peaks, waiting, waiting, for that malign head to appear above the window sills. More than that, a full half the time the head did appear—at least, I could have sworn I saw it. My muscles were rigid, my nerves were zooming with a horrible intensity, my eyes throbbed with the pain of their protrusion. I cursed Henry James, my "Beast in the Jungle" friend, my debonair London book-seller. I ached thoroughly for those days of comparative peace when I knew no more of Henry than that he was the brother of William, when Alps were beautiful white Alps and not red-headed evil butlers, and when the fate of little children was a problem academic pure and simple. I was thoroughly badly off. If somebody had come along to tell me of the catharsis value of tragedy, or the ennobling effect of participating in a dignified horror, I would surely have landed him at the foot of my steepest Alp.

But a very odd thing was to happen to me. I was to learn a very important lesson from "The Turn of the Screw," and it has stood me in good stead on many a day and night since. Along about the third night that my clammy obsession waked me, and I gaped dry-throated at the face in my starry window, I suddenly remembered that "The Turn of the Screw" had been written a fair number of years before I had ever read it, and that hundreds, probably thousands, of other unfortunates had stared at that same face in hundreds, probably thousands, of other windows. It was the most healing notion I ever had. In fact, I laughed. I knew for a certainty that, Henry James or no Henry James, that wretched monster could hardly have been so multiform as to exist actually in all of those windows. All of us were on the instant preposterous together—preposterous and safe. Any one of us was in mortal danger—all of us together were a comic and protected company. That deadly face fell back

out of my individual high Alpine window as promptly
as if he had been a rag baby at Coney Island that I had
just hit with a well aimed rag ball. All at once I knew
why we do cling together, even if sight unseen. I could
even understand why we sometimes behave so badly,
when we huddle. We can do anything, we must do anything, rather than try to go it alone, with our helpless
and terrified loneliness clutching at us in the night. It is
of course just possible that Henry James wrote "The
Turn of the Screw" to help us to discover this. It is also
possible that he wrote it for some quite different reason,
which will be fathomed in time for inclusion in some
different preface. Many prefaces will certainly be written,
many editions made, before "The Turn of the Screw"
will have spent its capacity to conscript the human
imagination.

HEYWOOD BROUN.

NEW YORK,
    January, 1930

THE TURN OF THE SCREW

THE TURN OF THE SCREW

THE story had held us, round the fire, sufficiently breathless, but except the obvious remark that it was gruesome, as, on Christmas eve in an old house, a strange tale should essentially be, I remember no comment uttered till somebody happened to say that it was the only case he had met in which such a visitation had fallen on a child. The case, I may mention, was that of an apparition in just such an old house as had gathered us for the occasion—an appearance, of a dreadful kind, to a little boy sleeping in the room with his mother and waking her up in the terror of it; waking her not to dissipate his dread and soothe him to sleep again, but to encounter also, herself, before she had succeeded in doing so, the same sight that had shaken him. It was this observation that drew from Douglas—not immediately, but later in the evening—a reply that had the interesting consequence to which I call attention. Someone else told a story not particularly effective, which I saw he was not following. This I took for a sign that he had himself something to produce and that we should only have to wait. We waited in fact till two nights later; but that same evening, before we scattered, he brought out what was in his mind.

"I quite agree—in regard to Griffin's ghost, or whatever it was—that its appearing first to the little boy, at so tender an age, adds a particular touch. But it's not the first occurrence of its charming kind that I know to have involved a child. If the child gives the effect another turn of the screw, what do you say to *two* children——?"

"We say, of course" somebody exclaimed, "that they

give two turns! Also that we want to hear about them."

I can see Douglas there before the fire, to which he had got up to present his back, looking down at his interlocutor with his hands in his pockets. "Nobody but me, till now, has ever heard. It's quite too horrible." This, naturally, was declared by several voices to give the thing the utmost price, and our friend, with quiet art, prepared his triumph by turning his eyes over the rest of us and going on: "It's beyond everything. Nothing at all that I know touches it."

"For sheer terror?" I remember asking.

He seemed to say it was not so simple as that; to be really at a loss how to qualify it. He passed his hand over his eyes, made a little wincing grimace. "For dreadful—dreadfulness!"

"Oh, how delicious!" cried one of the women.

He took no notice of her; he looked at me, but as if, instead of me, he saw what he spoke of. "For general uncanny ugliness and horror and pain."

"Well then," I said, "just sit right down and begin."

He turned round to the fire, gave a kick to a log, watched it an instant. Then as he faced us again: "I can't begin. I shall have to send to town." There was a unanimous groan at this, and much reproach; after which, in his preoccupied way, he explained. "The story's written. It's in a locked drawer—it has not been out for years. I could write to my man and enclose the key; he could send down the packet as he finds it." It was to me in particular that he appeared to propound this—appeared almost to appeal for aid not to hesitate. He had broken a thickness of ice, the formation of many a winter; had had his reasons for a long silence. The others resented postponement, but it was just his scruples that charmed me. I adjured him to write by the first post and to agree with us for an early hearing; then I asked him if the experience in question had been his own. To this his answer was prompt. "Oh, thank God, no!"

"And is the record yours? You took the thing down?"

"Nothing but the impression. I took that *here*"—he tapped his heart. "I've never lost it."

"Then your manuscript——?"

"Is in old, faded ink, and in the most beautiful hand." He hung fire again. "A woman's. She has been dead these twenty years. She sent me the pages in question before she died." They were all listening now, and of course there was somebody to be arch, or at any rate to draw the inference. But if he put the inference by without a smile it was also without irritation. "She was a most charming person, but she was ten years older than I. She was my sister's governess," he quietly said. "She was the the most agreeable woman I've ever known in her position; she would have been worthy of any whatever. It was long ago, and this episode was long before. I was at Trinity, and I found her at home on my coming down the second summer. I was much there that year—it was a beautiful one; and we had, in her off-hours, some strolls and talks in the garden—talks in which she struck me as awfully clever and nice. Oh yes; don't grin: I liked her extremely and am glad to this day to think she liked me too. If she hadn't she wouldn't have told me. She had never told anyone. It wasn't simply that she said so, but that I knew she hadn't. I was sure; I could see. You'll easily judge why when you hear."

"Because the thing had been such a scare?"

He continued to fix me. "You'll easily judge," he repeated: "*you* will."

I fixed him too. "I see. She was in love."

He laughed for the first time. "You *are* acute. Yes, she was in love. That is, she had been. That came out—she couldn't tell her story without its coming out. I saw it, and she saw I saw it; but neither of us spoke of it. I remember the time and the place—the corner of the lawn, the shade of the great beeches and the long, hot summer afternoon. It wasn't a scene for a shudder; but oh——!" He quitted the fire and dropped back into his chair.

"You'll receive the packet Thursday morning?" I inquired.

"Probably not till the second post."

"Well then; after dinner——"

"You'll all meet me here?" He looked us round again. "Isn't anybody going?" It was almost the tone of hope.

"Everybody will stay!"

"*I* will—and *I* will!" cried the ladies whose departure had been fixed. Mrs. Griffin, however, expressed the need for a little more light. "Who was it she was in love with?"

"The story will tell," I took upon myself to reply.

"Oh, I can't wait for the story!"

"The story *won't* tell," said Douglas; "not in any literal, vulgar way."

"More's the pity, then. That's the only way I ever understand."

"Won't *you* tell, Douglas?" somebody else inquired.

He sprang to his feet again. "Yes—tomorrow. Now I must go to bed. Good-night." And quickly catching up a candlestick, he left us slightly bewildered. From our end of the great brown hall we heard his step on the stair; whereupon Mrs. Griffin spoke. "Well, if I don't know who she was in love with, I know who *he* was."

"She was ten years older," said her husband.

"*Raison de plus*—at that age! But it's rather nice, his long reticence."

"Forty years!" Griffin put in.

"With this outbreak at last."

"The outbreak," I returned, "will make a tremendous occasion of Thursday night;" and everyone so agreed with me that, in the light of it, we lost all attention for everything else. The last story, however incomplete and like the mere opening of a serial, had been told; we handshook and "candlestuck," as somebody said, and went to bed.

I knew the next day that a letter containing the key had, by the first post, gone off to his London apartments; but in spite of—or perhaps just on account of—the eventual diffusion of this knowledge we quite let him alone till after dinner, till such an hour of the evening, in fact, as might best accord with the kind of emotion on which our hopes were fixed. Then he became as communicative as we could desire and indeed gave us his best reason for being so. We had it from him again before the fire in the hall, as we had had our mild wonders of the previous night. It appeared that the narrative he had promised to read us really required for a proper intelligence a few words of prologue. Let me say here distinctly, to have done with it, that this narrative, from an exact transcript of my own made much later, is what I shall presently give. Poor Douglas, before his death—when it was in sight—committed to me the manuscript that reached him on the third of these days and that, on the same spot, with immense effect, he began to read to our hushed little circle on the night of the fourth. The departing ladies who had said they would stay didn't, of course, thank heaven, stay: they departed, in consequence of arrangements made, in a rage of curiosity, as they professed, produced by the touches with which he had already worked us up. But that only made his little final auditory more compact and select, kept it, round the hearth, subject to a common thrill.

The first of these touches conveyed that the written statement took up the tale at a point after it had, in a manner, begun. The fact to be in possession of was therefore that his old friend, the youngest of several daughters of a poor country parson, had, at the age of twenty, on taking service for the first time in the schoolroom, come up to London, in trepidation, to answer in person an advertisement that had already placed her in brief correspondence with the advertiser. This person proved, on her presenting herself, for judgment, at a house in Harley Street, that impressed her as vast and imposing—this prospective patron proved a gentleman, a bachelor in the prime of life, such a figure as had never risen, save in a dream or an old novel, before a fluttered, anxious girl out of a Hampshire vicarage. One could easily fix his type; it never, happily, dies out. He was handsome and bold and pleasant, off-hand and gay and kind. He struck her, inevitably, as gallant and splendid, but what took her most of all and gave her the courage she afterwards showed was that he put the whole thing to her as a kind of favour, an obligation he should gratefully incur. She conceived him as rich, but as fearfully extravagant—saw him all in a glow of high fashion, of good looks, of expensive habits, of charming ways with women. He had for his own town residence a big house filled with the spoils of travel and the trophies of the chase; but it was to his country home. an old family place in Essex, that he wished her immediately to proceed.

He had been left, by the death of their parents in India, guardian to a small nephew and a small niece, children of a younger, a military brother, whom he had lost two years before. These children were, by the strangest of chances for a man in his position,—a lone man without the right sort of experience or a grain of patience,—very heavily on his hands. It had all been a great worry and, on his own part doubtless, a series of blunders, but he immensely pitied the poor chicks and had done all he could: had in particular sent them down to his other house, the proper place for them being of course the country, and kept them there, from the first, with the best people he could find to look after them, parting even with his own servants to wait on them and going down himself, whenever he might, to see how they were doing. The awkward thing was that they had practically no other relations and that his own affairs took up all his time. He had put them in possession of Bly, which was healthy and secure, and had placed at the head of their little establishment—but below stairs only—an excellent woman, Mrs. Grose, whom he was sure his visitor would like and who had formerly been maid to his mother. She was now housekeeper and was also acting for the time as superintendent to the little girl, of whom, without children of her own, she was, by good luck, extremely fond. There were plenty of people to help, but of course the young lady who should go down as governess would be in supreme authority. She would also have, in holidays, to look after the small boy, who had been for a term at school—young as he was to be sent, but what else could be done?—and who, as the holidays were about to begin, would be back from one day to the other. There had been for the two children at first a young lady whom they had had the misfortune to lose. She had done for them quite beautifully—she was a most respectable person—till her death, the great awkwardness of which had, precisely, left no alternative but the school for little Miles. Mrs. Grose, since then, in the way of manners and things, had done as she could for Flora; and there were, further, a cook, a housemaid, a dairywoman, an old pony, an old groom, and an old gardener, all likewise thoroughly respectable.

So far had Douglas presented his picture when someone put a question. "And what did the former governess die of?—of so much respectability?"

Our friend's answer was prompt. "That will come out. I don't anticipate."

"Excuse me—I thought that was just what you *are* doing."

"In her successor's place," I suggested, "I should have wished to learn if the office brought with it——"

"Necessary danger to life?" Douglas completed my thought. "She did wish to learn, and she did learn. You shall hear tomorrow what she learnt. Meanwhile, of course, the prospect struck her as slightly grim. She was young, untried, nervous: it was a vision of serious duties and little company, of really great loneliness. She hesitated—took a couple of days to consult and consider. But the salary offered much exceeded her modest measure, and on a second interview she faced the music, she engaged." And Douglas, with this, made a pause that, for the benefit of the company, moved me to throw in—

"The moral of which was of course the seduction exercised by the splendid young man. She succumbed to it."

He got up and, as he had done the night before, went to the fire, gave a stir to a log with his foot, then stood a moment with his back to us. "She saw him only twice."

"Yes, but that's just the beauty of her passion."

A little to my surprise, on this, Douglas turned round to me. "It *was* the beauty of it. There were others," he went on, "who hadn't succumbed. He told her frankly all his difficulty—that for several applicants the conditions had been prohibitive. They were, somehow, simply afraid. It sounded dull—it sounded strange; and all the more so because of his main condition."

"Which was——?"

"That she should never trouble him—but never, never: neither appeal nor complain nor write about anything; only meet all questions herself, receive all moneys from his solicitor, take the whole thing over and let him alone. She promised to do this, and she mentioned to me that when, for a moment, disburdened, delighted, he held her hand, thanking her for the sacrifice, she already felt rewarded."

"But was that all her reward?" one of the ladies asked.

"She never saw him again."

"Oh!" said the lady; which, as our friend immediately left us again, was the only other word of importance contributed to the subject till, the next night, by the corner of the hearth, in the best chair, he opened the faded red cover of a thin old-fashioned gilt-edged album. The whole thing took indeed more nights than one, but on the first occasion the same lady put another question. "What is your title?"

"I haven't one."

"Oh, *I* have!" I said. But Douglas, without heeding me, had begun to read with a fine clearness that was like a rendering to the ear of the beauty of his author's hand.

I

I REMEMBER the whole beginning as a succession of flights and drops, a little see-saw of the right throbs and the wrong. After rising, in town, to meet his appeal, I had at all events a couple of very bad days—found myself doubtful again, felt indeed sure I had made a mistake. In this state of mind I spent the long hours of bumping, swinging coach that carried me to the stopping-place at which I was to be met by a vehicle from the house. This convenience, I was told, had been ordered, and I found, toward the close of the June afternoon, a commodious fly in waiting for me. Driving at that hour, on a lovely day, through a country to which the summer sweetness seemed to offer me a friendly welcome, my fortitude mounted afresh and, as we turned into the avenue, encountered a reprieve that was probably but a proof of the point to which it had sunk. I suppose I had expected, or had dreaded, something so melancholy that what greeted me was a good surprise. I remember as a most pleasant impression the broad, clear front, its open windows and fresh curtains and the pair of maids looking out; I remember the lawn and the bright flowers and the crunch of my wheels on the gravel and the clustered treetops over which the rooks circled and cawed in the golden sky. The scene had a greatness that made it a different affair from my own scant home, and there immediately appeared at the door, with a little girl in her hand, a civil person who dropped me as decent a curtsey as if I had been the mistress or a distinguished visitor. I had received in Harley Street a narrower notion of the place, and that, as I recalled it, made me think the proprietor still more of a gentleman, suggested that what I was to enjoy might be something beyond his promise.

I had no drop again till the next day, for I was carried triumphantly through the following hours by my introduction to the younger of my pupils. The little girl who accompanied Mrs. Grose appeared to me on the spot a creature so charming as to make it a great fortune to have to do with her. She was the most beautiful child I had ever seen, and I afterwards wondered that my employer had not told me more of her. I slept little that night—I was too much excited; and this astonished me too, I recollect, remained with me, adding to my sense of the liberality with which I was treated. The large, impressive room, one of the best in the house, the great state bed, as I almost felt it, the full, figured draperies, the long glasses in which, for the first time, I could see myself from head to foot, all struck me—like the extraordinary charm of my small charge—as so many things thrown in. It was thrown in as well, from the first moment, that I should get on with Mrs. Grose in a relation over which, on my way, in the coach, I fear I had rather brooded. The only thing indeed that in this early outlook might have made me shrink again was the clear circumstance of her being so glad to see me. I perceived within half an hour that she was so glad—stout, simple, plain, clean, wholesome woman—as to be positively on her guard against showing it too much. I wondered even then a little why she should wish not to show it, and that, with reflection, with suspicion, might of course have made me uneasy.

But it was a comfort that there could be no uneasiness in a connection with anything so beatific as the radiant image of my little girl, the vision of whose angelic beauty had probably more than anything else to do with the restlessness that, before morning, made me several times rise and wander about my room to take in the whole picture and prospect; to watch, from my open window, the faint summer dawn, to look at such portions of the rest of the house as I could catch, and to listen, while, in the fading dusk, the first birds began to twitter, for the possible recurrence of a sound or two, less natural and not without, but within, that I had fancied I heard. There had been a moment when I believed I recognised, faint and far, the cry of a child; there had been another when I found myself just consciously starting as at the passage, before my door, of a light footstep. But these fancies were not marked enough not to be thrown off, and it is only in the light, or the gloom, I should rather say, of other and subsequent matters that they now come back to me. To watch, teach, "form" little Flora would too evidently be the making of a happy and useful life. It had been agreed between us downstairs that after this first occasion I should have her as a matter of course at night, her small white bed being already arranged, to that end, in my room. What I had undertaken was the whole care of her, and she had remained, just this last time, with Mrs. Grose only as an effect of our consideration for my inevitable strangeness and her natural timidity. In spite of this timidity—which the child herself, in the oddest way in the world, had been perfectly frank and brave about, allowing it, without a sign of uncomfortable consciousness, with the deep, sweet serenity indeed of one of Raphael's holy infants, to be discussed, to be imputed to her and to determine us—I felt quite sure she would presently like me. It was part of what I already liked Mrs. Grose herself for, the pleasure I could see her feel in my admiration and wonder as I sat at supper with four tall candles and with my pupil, in a high chair and a bib, brightly facing me, between them, over bread and milk. There were naturally things that in Flora's presence could pass between us only as prodigious and gratified looks, obscure and roundabout allusions.

"And the little boy—does he look like her? Is he too so very remarkable?"

One wouldn't flatter a child. "Oh, Miss, *most* remarkable. If you think well of this one!"—and she stood there with a plate in her hand, beaming at our companion, who looked from one of us to the other with placid heavenly eyes that contained nothing to check us.

"Yes; if I do——?"

"You *will* be carried away by the little gentleman!"

"Well, that, I think, is what I came for—to be carried away. I'm afraid, however," I remember feeling the impulse to add, "I'm rather easily carried away. I was carried away in London!"

I can still see Mrs. Grose's broad face as she took this in. "In Harley Street?"

"In Harley Street."

"Well, Miss, you're not the first—and you won't be the last."

"Oh, I've no pretension," I could laugh, "to being the only one. My other pupil, at any rate, as I understand, comes back tomorrow?"

"Not tomorrow—Friday, Miss. He arrives, as you did, by the coach, under care of the guard, and is to be met by the same carriage."

I forthwith expressed that the proper as well as the pleasant and friendly thing would be therefore that on the arrival of the public conveyance I should be in waiting for him with his little sister; an idea in which Mrs. Grose concurred so heartily that I somehow took her manner as a kind of comforting pledge—never falsified, thank heaven!—that we should on every question be quite at one. Oh, she was glad I was there!

What I felt the next day was, I suppose, nothing that could be fairly called a reaction from the cheer of my arrival; it was probably at the most only a slight oppression produced by a fuller measure of the scale, as I walked round them, gazed up at them, took them in, of my new circumstances. They had, as it were, an extent and mass for which I had not been prepared and in the presence of which I found myself, freshly, a little scared as well as a little proud. Lessons, in this agitation, certainly suffered some delay; I reflected that my first duty was, by the gentlest arts I could contrive, to win the child into the sense of knowing me. I spent the day with her out of doors; I arranged with her, to her great satisfaction, that it should be she, she only, who might show me the place. She showed it step by step and room by room and secret by secret, with droll, delightful, childish talk about it and with the result, in half an hour, of our becoming immense friends. Young as she was, I was struck, throughout our little tour, with her confidence and courage with the way, in empty chambers and dull corridors, on crooked staircases that made me pause and even on the summit of an old machicolated square tower that made me dizzy, her morning music, her disposition to tell me so many more things than she asked, rang out and led me on. I have not seen Bly since the day I left it, and I dare say that to my older and more informed eyes it would now appear sufficiently contracted. But as my little conductress, with her hair of gold and her frock of blue, danced before me round corners and pattered down passages, I had the view of a castle of romance inhabited by a rosy sprite, such a place as would somehow, for diversion of the young idea, take all colour out of storybooks and fairy-tales. Wasn't it just a storybook over which I had fallen a-doze and a-dream? No; it was a big, ugly, antique, but convenient house, embodying a few features of a building still older, half replaced and half utilised, in which I had the fancy of our being almost as lost as a handful of passengers in a great drifting ship Well, I was, strangely, at the helm!

II

THIS came home to me when, two days later, I drove over with Flora to meet, as Mrs. Grose said, the little gentleman; and all the more for an incident that, presenting itself the second evening, had deeply disconcerted me. The first day had been, on the whole, as I have expressed, reassuring; but I was to see it wind up in keen apprehension. The postbag, that evening,—it came late,—contained a letter for me, which, however, in the hand of my employer, I found to be composed but of a few words enclosing another, addressed to himself, with a seal still unbroken. "This, I recognise, is from the head-master, and the head-master's an awful bore. Read him, please; deal with him; but mind you don't report. Not a word. I'm off!" I broke the seal with a great effort—so great a one that I was a long time coming to it; took the unopened missive at last up to my room and only attacked it just before going to bed. I had better have let it wait till morning, for it gave me a second sleepless night. With no counsel to take, the next day, I was full of distress; and it finally got so the better of me that I determined to open myself at least to Mrs. Grose.

"What does it mean? The child's dismissed his school."

She gave me a look that I remarked at the moment; then, visibly, with a quick blankness, seemed to try to take it back. "But aren't they all——?"

"Sent home—yes. But only for the holidays. Miles may never go back at all."

Consciously, under my attention, she reddened. "They won't take him?"

"They absolutely decline."

At this she raised her eyes, which she had turned from

me; I saw them fill with good tears. "What has he done?"

I hesitated; then I judged best simply to hand her my letter—which, however, had the effect of making her, without taking it, simply put her hands behind her. She shook her head sadly. "Such things are not for me, Miss."

My counsellor couldn't read! I winced at my mistake, which I attenuated as I could, and opened my letter again to repeat it to her; then, faltering in the act and folding it up once more, I put it back in my pocket. "Is he really *bad?*"

The tears were still in her eyes. "Do the gentlemen say so?"

"They go into no particulars. They simply express their regret that it should be impossible to keep him. That can have only one meaning." Mrs. Grose listened with dumb emotion; she forbore to ask me what this meaning might be; so that, presently, to put the thing with some coherence and with the mere aid of her presence to my own mind, I went on: "That he's an injury to the others."

At this, with one of the quick turns of simple folk, she suddenly flamed up. "Master Miles! *him* an injury?"

There was such a flood of good faith in it that, though I had not yet seen the child, my very fears made me jump to the absurdity of the idea. I found myself, to meet my friend the better, offering it, on the spot, sarcastically. "To his poor little innocent mates!"

"It's too dreadful," cried Mrs. Grose, "to say such cruel things! Why, he's scarce ten years old."

"Yes, yes; it would be incredible."

She was evidently grateful for such a profession. "See him, Miss, first. *Then* believe it!" I felt forthwith a new impatience to see him; it was the beginning of a curiosity that, for all the next hours, was to deepen almost to pain. Mrs. Grose was aware, I could judge, of what she had produced in me, and she followed it up with assurance. "You might as well believe it of the little lady. Bless her," she added the next moment—"*look* at her!"

I turned and saw that Flora, whom, ten minutes before, I had established in the schoolroom with a sheet of white paper, a pencil, and a copy of nice "round O's," now presented herself to view at the open door. She expressed in her little way an extraordinary detachment from disagreeable duties, looking to me, however, with a great childish light that seemed to offer it as a mere result of the affection she had conceived for my person, which had rendered necessary that she should follow me. I needed nothing more than this to feel the full force of Mrs. Grose's comparison, and, catching my pupil in my arms, covered her with kisses in which there was a sob of atonement.

None the less, the rest of the day, I watched for further occasion to approach my colleague, especially as, toward evening, I began to fancy she rather sought to avoid me. I overtook her, I remember, on the staircase; we went down together, and at the bottom I detained her, holding her there with a hand on her arm. "I take what you said to me at noon as a declaration that *you've* never known him to be bad."

She threw back her head; she had clearly, by this time, and very honestly, adopted an attitude. "Oh, never known him—I don't pretend *that!*"

I was upset again. "Then you *have* known him——?"

"Yes indeed, Miss, thank God!"

On reflection I accepted this. "You mean that a boy who never is——?"

"Is no boy for *me!*"

I held her tighter. "You like them with the spirit to be naughty?" Then, keeping pace with her answer, "So do I!" I eagerly brought out. "But not to the degree to contaminate——"

"To contaminate?"—my big word left her at a loss. I explained it. "To corrupt."

She stared, taking my meaning in; but it produced in her an odd laugh. "Are you afraid he'll corrupt *you?*" She put the question with such a fine bold humour that, with a laugh, a little silly doubtless, to match her own, I gave way for the time to the apprehension of ridicule.

But the next day, as the hour for my drive approached, I cropped up in another place. "What was the lady who was here before?"

"The last governess? She was also young and pretty—almost as young and almost as pretty, Miss, even as you."

"Ah, then, I hope her youth and her beauty helped her!" I recollect throwing off. "He seems to like us young and pretty!"

"Oh, he *did*," Mrs. Grose assented: "it was the way he liked everyone!" She had no sooner spoken indeed than she caught herself up. "I mean that's *his* way—the master's."

I was struck. "But of whom did you speak first?"

She looked blank, but she coloured. "Why, of *him*."

"Of the master?"

"Of who else?"

There was so obviously no one else that the next moment I had lost my impression of her having accidentally said more than she meant; and I merely asked what I wanted to know. "Did *she* see anything in the boy——?"

"That wasn't right? She never told me."

I had a scruple, but I overcame it. "Was she careful—particular?"

Mrs. Grose appeared to try to be conscientious. "About some things—yes."

"But not about all?"

Again she considered. "Well, Miss—she's gone. I won't tell tales."

"I quite understand your feeling," I hastened to reply; but I thought it, after an instant, not opposed to this concession to pursue: "Did she die here?"

"No—she went off."

I don't know what there was in this brevity of Mrs. Grose's that struck me as ambiguous. "Went off to die?"

Mrs. Grose looked straight out of the window, but I felt

that, hypothetically, I had a right to know what young persons engaged for Bly were expected to do. "She was taken ill, you mean, and went home?"

"She was not taken ill, so far as appeared, in this house. She left it, at the end of the year, to go home, as she said, for a short holiday, to which the time she had put in had certainly given her a right. We had then a young woman —a nursemaid who had stayed on and who was a good girl and clever; and *she* took the children altogether for the interval. But our young lady never came back, and at the very moment I was expecting her I heard from the master that she was dead."

I turned this over. "But of what?"

"He never told me! But please, Miss," said Mrs. Grose, "I must get to my work."

III

Her thus turning her back on me was fortunately not, for my just preoccupations, a snub that could check the growth of our mutual esteem. We met, after I had brought home little Miles, more intimately than ever on the ground of my stupefaction, my general emotion: so monstrous was I then ready to pronounce it that such a child as had now been revealed to me should be under an interdict. I was a little late on the scene, and I felt, as he stood wistfully looking out for me before the door of the inn at which the coach had put him down, that I had seen him, on the instant, without and within, in the great glow of freshness, the same positive fragrance of purity, in which I had, from the first moment, seen his little sister. He was incredibly beautiful, and Mrs. Grose had put her finger on it: everything but a sort of passion of tenderness for him was swept away by his presence. What I then and there took him to my heart for was something divine that I have never found to the same degree in any child—his indescribable little air of knowing nothing in the world but love. It would have been impossible to carry a bad name with a greater sweetness of innocence, and by the time I had got back to Bly with him I remained merely bewildered—so far, that is, as I was not outraged—by the sense of the horrible letter locked up in my room, in a drawer. As soon as I could compass a private word with Mrs. Grose I declared to her that it was grotesque.

She promptly understood me. "You mean the cruel charge——?"

"It doesn't live an instant. My dear woman, *look* at him!"

She smiled at my pretension to have discovered his

charm. "I assure you, Miss, I do nothing else! What will you say, then?" she immediately added.

"In answer to the letter?" I had made up my mind. "Nothing."

"And to his uncle?"

I was incisive. "Nothing."

"And to the boy himself?"

I was wonderful. "Nothing."

She gave with her apron a great wipe to her mouth. "Then I'll stand by you. We'll see it out."

"We'll see it out!" I ardently echoed, giving her my hand to make it a vow.

She held me there a moment, then whisked up her apron again with her detached hand. "Would you mind, Miss, if I used the freedom——"

"To kiss me? No!" I took the good creature in my arms and, after we had embraced like sisters, felt still more fortified and indignant.

This, at all events, was for the time: a time so full that, as I recall the way it went, it reminds me of all the art I now need to make it a little distinct. What I look back at with amazement is the situation I accepted. I had undertaken, with my companion, to see it out, and I was under a charm, apparently, that could smooth away the extent and the far and difficult connections of such an effort. I was lifted aloft on a great wave of infatuation and pity. I found it simple, in my ignorance, my confusion, and perhaps my conceit, to assume that I could deal with a boy whose education for the world was all on the point of beginning. I am unable even to remember at this day what proposal I framed for the end of his holidays and the resumption of his studies. Lessons with me, indeed, that charming summer, we all had a theory that he was to have; but I now feel that, for weeks, the lessons must have been rather my own. I learnt something—at first certainly—that had not been one of the teachings of my small, smothered life; learnt to be amused, and even amusing, and not to think for the morrow. It was the first time, in a manner, that I had known space and air and freedom, all the music of summer and all the mystery of nature. And then there was consideration—and consideration was sweet. Oh, it was a trap—not designed, but deep —to my imagination, to my delicacy, perhaps to my vanity; to whatever, in me, was most excitable. The best way to picture it all is to say that I was off my guard. They gave me so little trouble—they were of a gentleness so extraordinary. I used to speculate—but even this with a dim disconnectedness—as to how the rough future (for all futures are rough!) would handle them and might bruise them. They had the bloom of health and happiness; and yet, as if I had been in charge of a pair of little grandees, of princes of the blood, for whom everything, to be right, would have to be enclosed and protected, the only form that, in my fancy, the after-years could take for them was that of a romantic, a really royal extension of the garden and the park. It may be, of course, above all, that what suddenly broke into this gives the previous time a charm of stillness—that hush in which something gathers or crouches. The change was actually like the spring of a beast.

In the first weeks the days were long; they often, at their finest, gave me what I used to call my own hour, the hour when, for my pupils, tea-time and bed-time having come and gone, I had, before my final retirement, a small interval alone. Much as I liked my companions, this hour was the thing in the day I liked most; and I liked it best of all when, as the light faded—or rather, I should say, the day lingered and the last calls of the last birds sounded, in a flushed sky, from the old trees—I could take a turn into the grounds and enjoy, almost with a sense of property that amused and flattered me, the beauty and dignity of the place. It was a pleasure at these moments to feel myself tranquil and justified; doubtless, perhaps, also to reflect that by my discretion, my quiet good sense and

general high propriety, I was giving pleasure—if he ever
thought of it!—to the person to whose pressure I had
responded. What I was doing was what he had earnestly
hoped and directly asked of me, and that I *could*, after
all, do it proved even a greater joy than I had expected.
I dare say I fancied myself, in short, a remarkable young
woman and took comfort in the faith that this would
more publicly appear. Well, I needed to be remarkable to
offer a front to the remarkable things that presently gave
their first sign.

It was plump, one afternoon, in the middle of my very
hour: the children were tucked away and I had come out
for my stroll. One of the thoughts that, as I don't in the
least shrink now from noting, used to be with me in these
wanderings was that it would be as charming as a charming story suddenly to meet someone. Someone would
appear there at the turn of a path and would stand before
me and smile and approve. I didn't ask more than that—
I only asked that he should *know* ; and the only way to be
sure he knew would be to see it, and the kind light of it,
in his handsome face. That was exactly present to me—
by which I mean the face was—when, on the first of these
occasions, at the end of a long June day, I stopped short
on emerging from one of the plantations and coming into
view of the house. What arrested me on the spot—and
with a shock much greater than any vision had allowed
for—was the sense that my imagination had, in a flash,
turned real. He did stand there!—but high up, beyond the
lawn and at the very top of the tower to which, on that
first morning, little Flora had conducted me. This tower
was one of a pair—square, incongruous, crenelated struc-
tures—that were distinguished, for some reason, though I
could see little difference, as the new and the old. They
flanked opposite ends of the house and were probably
architectural absurdities, redeemed in a measure indeed
by not being wholly disengaged nor of a height too preten-
tious, dating, in their gingerbread antiquity, from a

romantic revival that was already a respectable past. I
admired them, had fancies about them, for we could all
profit in a degree, especially when they loomed through
the dusk, by the grandeur of their actual battlements; yet
it was not at such an elevation that the figure I had so
often invoked seemed most in place.

It produced in me, this figure, in the clear twilight, I
remember, two distinct gasps of emotion, which were,
sharply, the shock of my first and that of my second surprise. My second was a violent perception of the mistake
of my first: the man who met my eyes was not the person
I had precipitately supposed. There came to me thus a
bewilderment of vision of which, after these years, there is
no living view that I can hope to give. An unknown man
in a lonely place is a permitted object of fear to a young
woman privately bred; and the figure that faced me was
—a few more seconds assured me—as little anyone else I
knew as it was the image that had been in my mind. I had
not seen it in Harley Street—I had not seen it anywhere.
The place, moreover, in the strangest way in the world,
had, on the instant, and by the very fact of its appearance,
become a solitude. To me at least, making my statement
here with a deliberation with which I have never made it,
the whole feeling of the moment returns. It was as if, while
I took in—what I did take in—all the rest of the scene
had been stricken with death. I can hear again, as I write,
the intense hush in which the sounds of evening dropped.
The rooks stopped cawing in the golden sky and the
friendly hour lost, for the minute, all its voice. But there
was no other change in nature, unless indeed it were a
change that I saw with a stranger sharpness. The gold
was still in the sky, the clearness in the air, and the man
who looked at me over the battlements was as definite as
a picture in a frame. That's how I thought, with extraordinary quickness, of each person that he might have been
and that he was not. We were confronted across our distance quite long enough for me to ask myself with in-

tensity who then he was and to feel, as an effect of my inability to say, a wonder that in a few instants more became intense.

The great question, or one of these, is, afterwards, I know, with regard to certain matters, the question of how long they have lasted. Well, this matter of mine, think what you will of it, lasted while I caught at a dozen possibilities, none of which made a difference for the better, that I could see, in there having been in the house —and for how long, above all?—a person of whom I was in ignorance. It lasted while I just bridled a little with the sense that my office demanded that there should be no such ignorance and no such person. It lasted while this visitant, at all events,—and there was a touch of the strange freedom, as I remember, in the sign of familiarity of his wearing no hat,—seemed to fix me, from his position, with just the question, just the scrutiny through the fading light, that his own presence provoked. We were too far apart to call to each other, but there was a moment at which, at shorter range, some challenge between us, breaking the hush, would have been the right result of our straight mutual stare. He was in one of the angles, the one away from the house, very erect, as it struck me, and with both hands on the ledge. So I saw him as I see the letters I form on this page; then, exactly, after a minute, as if to add to the spectacle, he slowly changed his place— passed, looking at me hard all the while, to the opposite corner of the platform. Yes, I had the sharpest sense that during this transit he never took his eyes from me, and I can see at this moment the way his hand, as he went, passed from one of the crenelations to the next. He stopped at the other corner, but less long, and even as he turned away still markedly fixed me. He turned away; that was all I knew.

IV

IT was not that I didn't wait, on this occasion, for more,
for I was rooted as deeply as I was shaken. Was there a
"secret" at Bly—a mystery of Udolpho or an insane, an
unmentionable relative kept in unsuspected confinement?
I can't say how long I turned it over, or how long, in a
confusion of curiosity and dread, I remained where I had
had my collision; I only recall that when I re-entered the
house darkness had quite closed in. Agitation, in the
interval, certainly had held me and driven me, for I must,
in circling about the place, have walked three miles; but
I was to be, later on, so much more overwhelmed that this
mere dawn of alarm was a comparatively human chill.
The most singular part of it in fact—singular as the rest
had been—was the part I became, in the hall, aware of in
meeting Mrs. Grose. This picture comes back to me in
the general train—the impression, as I received it on my
return, of the wide white panelled space, bright in the
lamplight and with its portraits and red carpet, and of the
good surprised look of my friend, which immediately told
me she had missed me. It came to me straightway, under
her contact, that, with plain heartiness, mere relieved
anxiety at my appearance, she knew nothing whatever
that could bear upon the incident I had there ready for
her. I had not suspected in advance that her comfortable
face would pull me up, and I somehow measured the importance of what I had seen by my thus finding myself
hesitate to mention it. Scarce anything in the whole
history seems to me so odd as this fact that my real beginning of fear was one, as I may say, with the instinct of
sparing my companion. On the spot, accordingly, in the
pleasant hall and with her eyes on me, I, for a reason that

26

I couldn't then have phrased, achieved an inward revolution—offered a vague pretext for my lateness and, with the plea of the beauty of the night and of the heavy dew and wet feet, went as soon as possible to my room.

Here it was another affair; here, for many days after, it was a queer affair enough. There were hours, from day to day,—or at least there were moments, snatched even from clear duties,—when I had to shut myself up to think. It was not so much yet that I was more nervous than I could bear to be as that I was remarkably afraid of becoming so; for the truth I had now to turn over was, simply and clearly, the truth that I could arrive at no account whatever of the visitor with whom I had been so inexplicably and yet, as it seemed to me, so intimately concerned. It took little time to see that I could sound without forms of inquiry and without exciting remark any domestic complication. The shock I had suffered must have sharpened all my senses; I felt sure, at the end of three days and as the result of mere closer attention, that I had not been practised upon by the servants nor made the object of any "game." Of whatever it was that I knew nothing was known around me. There was but one sane inference: someone had taken a liberty rather gross. That was what, repeatedly, I dipped into my room and locked the door to say to myself. We had been, collectively, subject to an intrusion; some unscrupulous traveller, curious in old houses, had made his way in unobserved, enjoyed the prospect from the best point of view, and then stolen out as he came. If he had given me such a bold hard stare, that was but a part of his indiscretion. The good thing, after all, was that we should surely see no more of him.

This was not so good a thing, I admit, as not to leave me to judge that what, essentially, made nothing else much signify was simply my charming work. My charming work was just my life with Miles and Flora, and through nothing could I so like it as through feeling that

I could throw myself into it in trouble. The attraction of my small charges was a constant joy, leading me to wonder afresh at the vanity of my original fears, the distaste I had begun by entertaining for the probable grey prose of my office. There was to be no grey prose, it appeared, and no long grind; so how could work not be charming that presented itself as daily beauty? It was all the romance of the nursery and the poetry of the school-room. I don't mean by this, of course, that we studied only fiction and verse; I mean I can express no otherwise the sort of interest my companions inspired. How can I describe that except by saying that instead of growing used to them—and it's a marvel for a governess: I call the sisterhood to witness!—I made constant fresh discoveries. There was one direction, assuredly, in which these discoveries stopped: deep obscurity continued to cover the region of the boy's conduct at school. It had been promptly given me, I have noted, to face that mystery without a pang. Perhaps even it would be nearer the truth to say that—without a word—he himself had cleared it up. He had made the whole charge absurd. My conclusion bloomed there with the real rose-flush of his innocence: he was only too fine and fair for the little horrid, unclean school-world, and he had paid a price for it. I reflected acutely that the sense of such differences, such superiorities of quality, always, on the part of the majority—which could include even stupid, sordid head-masters—turns infallibly to the vindictive.

Both the children had a gentleness (it was their only fault, and it never made Miles a muff) that kept them—how shall I express it?—almost impersonal and certainly quite unpunishable. They were like the cherubs of the anecdote, who had—morally, at any rate—nothing to whack! I remember feeling with Miles in especial as if he had had, as it were, no history. We expect of a small child a scant one, but there was in this beautiful little boy something extraordinarily sensitive, yet extraordinarily

happy, that, more than in any creature of his age I have
seen, struck me as beginning anew each day. He had never
for a second suffered. I took this as a direct disproof of his
having really been chastised. If he had been wicked he
would have "caught" it, and I should have caught it by
the rebound—I should have found the trace. I found
nothing at all, and he was therefore angel. He never spoke
of his school, never mentioned a comrade or a master;
and I, for my part, was quite too much disgusted to allude
to them. Of course I was under the spell, and the wonderful part is that, even at the time, I perfectly knew I
was. But I gave myself up to it; it was an antidote to any
pain, and I had more pains than one. I was in receipt in
these days of disturbing letters from home, where things
were not going well. But with my children, what things in
the world mattered? That was the question I used to
put to my scrappy retirements. I was dazzled by their
loveliness.

There was a Sunday—to get on—when it rained with
such force and for so many hours that there could be no
procession to church; in consequence of which, as the day
declined, I had arranged with Mrs. Grose that, should the
evening show improvement, we would attend together the
late service. The rain happily stopped, and I prepared for
our walk, which, through the park and by the good road
to the village, would be a matter of twenty minutes.
Coming downstairs to meet my colleague in the hall, I
remembered a pair of gloves that had required three
stitches and that had received them—with a publicity
perhaps not edifying—while I sat with the children at
their tea, served on Sundays, by exception, in that cold,
clean temple of mahogany and brass, the "grown-up"
dining-room. The gloves had been dropped there, and I
turned in to recover them. The day was grey enough, but
the afternoon light still lingered, and it enabled me, on
crossing the threshold, not only to recognise, on a chair
near the wide window, then closed, the articles I wanted,

but to become aware of a person on the other side of the window and looking straight in. One step into the room had sufficed; my vision was instantaneous; it was all there. The person looking straight in was the person who had already appeared to me. He appeared thus again with I won't say greater distinctness, for that was impossible, but with a nearness that represented a forward stride in our intercourse and made me, as I met him, catch my breath and turn cold. He was the same—he was the same, and seen, this time, as he had been seen before, from the waist up, the window, though the dining-room was on the ground-floor, not going down to the terrace on which he stood. His face was close to the glass, yet the effect of this better view was, strangely, only to show me how intense the former had been. He remained but a few seconds—long enough to convince me he also saw and recognised; but it was as if I had been looking at him for years and had known him always. Something, however, happened this time that had not happened before; his stare into my face, through the glass and across the room, was as deep and hard as then, but it quitted me for a moment during which I could still watch it, see it fix successively several other things. On the spot there came to me the added shock of a certitude that it was not for me he had come there. He had come for someone else.

The flash of this knowledge—for it was knowledge in the midst of dread—produced in me the most extraordinary effect, started, as I stood there, a sudden vibration of duty and courage. I say courage because I was beyond all doubt already far gone. I bounded straight out of the door again, reached that of the house, got, in an instant, upon the drive, and, passing along the terrace as fast as I could rush, turned a corner and came full in sight. But it was in sight of nothing now—my visitor had vanished. I stopped, I almost dropped, with the real relief of this; but I took in the whole scene—I gave him time to reappear. I call it time, but how long was it? I can't speak to the purpose today of the duration of these things. That kind of measure must have left me: they couldn't have lasted as they actually appeared to me to last. The terrace and the whole place, the lawn and the garden beyond it, all I could see of the park, were empty with a great emptiness. There were shrubberies and big trees, but I remember the clear assurance I felt that none of them concealed him. He was there or was not there: not there if I didn't see him. I got hold of this; then, instinctively, instead of returning as I had come, went to the window. It was confusedly present to me that I ought to place myself where he had stood. I did so; I applied my face to the pane and looked, as he had looked, into the room. As if, at this moment, to show me exactly what his range had been, Mrs. Grose, as I had done for himself just before, came in from the hall. With this I had the full image of a repetition of what had already occurred. She saw me as I had seen my own visitant; she pulled up short as I had done; I gave her something of the shock that I had received. She turned white, and this made me ask myself if I had blanched as much. She stared, in short, and retreated on just *my* lines, and I knew she had then passed out and come round to me and that I should presently meet her. I remained where I was, and while I waited I thought of more things than one. But there's only one I take space to mention. I wondered why *she* should be scared.

V

Oh, she let me know as soon as, round the corner of the house, she loomed again into view. "What in the name of goodness is the matter——?" She was now flushed and out of breath.

I said nothing till she came quite near. "With me?" I must have made a wonderful face. "Do I show it?"

"You're as white as a sheet. You look awful."

I considered; I could meet on this, without scruple, any innocence. My need to respect the bloom of Mrs. Grose's had dropped, without a rustle, from my shoulders, and if I wavered for the instant it was not with what I kept back. I put out my hand to her and she took it; I held her hard a little, liking to feel her close to me. There was a kind of support in the shy heave of her surprise. "You came for me for church, of course, but I can't go."

"Has anything happened?"

"Yes. You must know now. Did I look very queer?"

"Through this window? Dreadful!"

"Well," I said, "I've been frightened." Mrs. Grose's eyes expressed plainly that *she* had no wish to be, yet also that she knew too well her place not to be ready to share with me any marked inconvenience. Oh, it was quite settled that she *must* share! "Just what you saw from the dining-room a minute ago was the effect of that. What *I* saw—just before—was much worse."

Her hand tightened. "What was it?"

"An extraordinary man. Looking in."

"What extraordinary man?"

"I haven't the least idea."

Mrs. Grose gazed round us in vain. "Then where is he gone?"

"I know still less."

"Have you seen him before?"

"Yes—once. On the old tower."

She could only look at me harder. "Do you mean he's a stranger?"

"Oh, very much!"

"Yet you didn't tell me?"

"No—for reasons. But now that you've guessed——"

Mrs. Grose's round eyes encountered this charge. "Ah, I haven't guessed!" she said very simply. "How can I if *you* don't imagine?"

"I don't in the very least."

"You've seen him nowhere but on the tower?"

"And on this spot just now."

Mrs. Grose looked round again. "What was he doing on the tower?"

"Only standing there and looking down at me."

She thought a minute. "Was he a gentleman?"

I found I had no need to think. "No." She gazed in deeper wonder. "No."

"Then nobody about the place? Nobody from the village?"

"Nobody—nobody. I didn't tell you, but I made sure."

She breathed a vague relief: this was, oddly, so much to the good. It only went indeed a little way. "But if he isn't a gentleman——"

"What *is* he? He's a horror."

"A horror?"

"He's—God help me if I know *what* he is!"

Mrs. Grose looked round once more; she fixed her eyes on the duskier distance, then, pulling herself together, turned to me with abrupt inconsequence. "It's time we should be at church."

"Oh, I'm not fit for church!"

"Won't it do you good?"

"It won't do *them*——!" I nodded at the house.

"The children?"

"I can't leave them now."

"You're afraid——?"

I spoke boldly. "I'm afraid of *him*."

Mrs. Grose's large face showed me, at this, for the first time, the far-away faint glimmer of a consciousness more acute: I somehow made out in it the delayed dawn of an idea I myself had not given her and that was as yet quite obscure to me. It comes back to me that I thought instantly of this as something I could get from her; and I felt it to be connected with the desire she presently showed to know more. "When was it—on the tower?"

"About the middle of the month. At this same hour."

"Almost at dark?" said Mrs. Grose.

"Oh, no, not nearly. I saw him as I see you."

"Then how did he get in?"

"And how did he get out?" I laughed. "I had no opportunity to ask him! This evening, you see," I pursued, "he has not been able to get in."

"He only peeps?"

"I hope it will be confined to that!" She had now let go my hand; she turned away a little. I waited an instant; then I brought out: "Go to church. Good-bye. I must watch."

Slowly she faced me again. "Do you fear for them?"

We met in another long look. "Don't *you?*" Instead of answering she came nearer to the window and, for a minute, applied her face to the glass. "You see how he could see," I meanwhile went on.

She didn't move. "How long was he here?"

"Till I came out. I came to meet him."

Mrs. Grose at last turned round, and there was still more in her face. "*I* couldn't have come out."

"Neither could I!" I laughed again. "But I did come. I have my duty."

"So have I mine," she replied; after which she added: "What is he like?"

"I've been dying to tell you. But he's like nobody."

"Nobody?" she echoed.

"He has no hat." Then seeing in her face that she already, in this, with a deeper dismay, found a touch of picture, I quickly added stroke to stroke. "He has red hair, very red, close-curling, and a pale face, long in shape, with straight, good features and little, rather queer whiskers that are as red as his hair. His eyebrows are, somehow, darker; they look particularly arched and as if they might move a good deal. His eyes are sharp, strange—awfully; but I only know clearly that they're rather small and very fixed. His mouth's wide, and his lips are thin, and except for his little whiskers he's quite clean-shaven. He gives me a sort of sense of looking like an actor."

"An actor!" It was impossible to resemble one *less*, at least, than Mrs. Grose at that moment.

"I've never seen one, but so I suppose them. He's tall, active, erect," I continued, "but never—no, never!—a gentleman."

My companion's face had blanched as I went on; her round eyes started and her mild mouth gaped. "A gentleman?" she gasped, confounded, stupefied: "a gentleman *he?*"

"You know him then?"

She visibly tried to hold herself. "But he *is* handsome?"

I saw the way to help her. "Remarkably!"

"And dressed——?"

"In somebody's clothes. They're smart, but they're not his own."

She broke into a breathless affirmative groan. "They're the master's!"

I caught it up. "You *do* know him?"

She faltered but a second. "Quint!" she cried.

"Quint?"

"Peter Quint—his own man, his valet, when he was here!"

"When the master was?"

Gaping still, but meeting me, she pieced it all together. "He never wore his hat, but he did wear—well, there were waistcoats missed! They were both here—last year. Then the master went, and Quint was alone."

I followed, but halting a little. "Alone?"

"Alone with *us*." Then, as from a deeper depth, "In charge," she added.

"And what became of him?"

She hung fire so long that I was still more mystified. "He went too," she brought out at last.

"Went where?"

Her expression, at this, became extraordinary. "God knows where! He died."

"Died?" I almost shrieked.

She seemed fairly to square herself, plant herself more firmly to utter the wonder of it. "Yes. Mr. Quint is dead."

VI

It took of course more than that particular passage to
place us together in presence of what we had now to live
with as we could—my dreadful liability to impressions of
the order so vividly exemplified, and my companion's
knowledge, henceforth,—a knowledge half consternation
and half compassion,—of that liability. There had been,
this evening, after the revelation that left me, for an
hour, so prostrate—there had been, for either of us, no
attendance on any service but a little service of tears and
vows, of prayers and promises, a climax to the series of
mutual challenges and pledges that had straightway
ensued on our retreating together to the schoolroom and
shutting ourselves up there to have everything out. The
result of our having everything out was simply to reduce
our situation to the last rigour of its elements. She herself
had seen nothing, not the shadow of a shadow, and nobody in the house but the governess was in the governess's
plight; yet she accepted without directly impugning my
sanity the truth as I gave it to her, and ended by showing
me, on this ground, an awe-stricken tenderness, an expression of the sense of my more than questionable privilege,
of which the very breath has remained with me as that
of the sweetest of human charities.

What was settled between us, accordingly, that night,
was that we thought we might bear things together; and
I was not even sure that, in spite of her exemption, it was
she who had the best of the burden. I knew at this hour, I
think, as well as I knew later what I was capable of
meeting to shelter my pupils; but it took me some time
to be wholly sure of what my honest ally was prepared
for to keep terms with so compromising a contract. I was

queer company enough—quite as queer as the company I received; but as I trace over what we went through I see how much common ground we must have found in the one idea that, by good fortune, *could* steady us. It was the idea, the second movement, that led me straight out, as I may say, of the inner chamber of my dread. I could take the air in the court, at least, and there Mrs. Grose could join me. Perfectly can I recall now the particular way strength came to me before we separated for the night. We had gone over and over every feature of what I had seen.

"He was looking for someone else, you say—someone who was not you?"

"He was looking for little Miles." A portentous clearness now possessed me. "*That's* whom he was looking for."

"But how do you know?"

"I know, I know, I know!" My exaltation grew. "And *you* know, my dear!"

She didn't deny this, but I required, I felt, not even so much telling as that. She resumed in a moment, at any rate: "What if *he* should see him?"

"Little Miles? That's what he wants!"

She looked immensely scared again. "The child?"

"Heaven forbid! The man. He wants to appear to *them*." That he might was an awful conception, and yet, somehow, I could keep it at bay; which, moreover, as we lingered there, was what I succeeded in practically proving. I had an absolute certainty that I could see again what I had already seen, but something within me said that by offering myself bravely as the sole subject of such experience, by accepting, by inviting, by surmounting it all, I should serve as an expiatory victim and guard the tranquillity of my companions. The children, in especial, I should thus fence about and absolutely save. I recall one of the last things I said that night to Mrs. Grose.

"It does strike me that my pupils have never mentioned——"

She looked at me hard as I musingly pulled up. "His having been here and the time they were with him?"

"The time they were with him, and his name, his presence, his history, in any way."

"Oh, the little lady doesn't remember. She never heard or knew."

"The circumstances of his death?" I thought with some intensity. "Perhaps not. But Miles would remember— Miles would know."

"Ah, don't try him!" broke from Mrs. Grose.

I returned her the look she had given me. "Don't be afraid." I continued to think. "It *is* rather odd."

"That he has never spoken of him?"

"Never by the least allusion. And you tell me they were 'great friends'?"

"Oh, it wasn't *him!*" Mrs. Grose with emphasis declared. "It was Quint's own fancy. To play with him, I mean—to spoil him." She paused a moment; then she added: "Quint was much too free."

This gave me, straight from my vision of his face—*such* a face!—a sudden sickness of disgust. "Too free with *my* boy?"

"Too free with everyone!"

I forebore, for the moment, to analyse this description further than by the reflection that a part of it applied to several of the members of the household, of the half-dozen maids and men who were still of our small colony. But there was everything, for our apprehension, in the lucky fact that no discomfortable legend, no perturbation of scullions, had ever, within anyone's memory, attached to the kind old place. It had neither bad name nor ill fame, and Mrs. Grose, most apparently, only desired to cling to me and to quake in silence. I even put her, the very last thing of all, to the test. It was when, at midnight, she had her hand on the schoolroom door to take leave. "I have it from you then—for it's of great importance—that he was definitely and admittedly bad?"

"Oh, not admittedly. *I* knew it—but the master didn't."

"And you never told him?"

"Well, he didn't like tale-bearing—he hated complaints. He was terribly short with anything of that kind, and if people were all right to *him*——"

"He wouldn't be bothered with more?" This squared well enough with my impression of him: he was not a trouble-loving gentleman, nor so very particular perhaps about some of the company *he* kept. All the same, I pressed my interlocutress. "I promise you *I* would have told!"

She felt my discrimination. "I dare say I was wrong. But, really, I was afraid."

"Afraid of what?"

"Of things that man could do. Quint was so clever—he was so deep."

I took this in still more than, probably, I showed. "You weren't afraid of anything else? Not of his effect——?"

"His effect?" she repeated with a face of anguish and waiting while I faltered.

"On innocent little precious lives. They were in your charge."

"No, they were not in mine!" she roundly and distressfully returned. "The master believed in him and placed him here because he was supposed not to be well and the country air so good for him. So he had everything to say. 'Yes"—she let me have it—"even about *them*."

"Them—that creature?" I had to smother a kind of howl. "And you could bear it!"

"No. I couldn't—and I can't now!" And the poor woman burst into tears.

A rigid control, from the next day, was, as I have said, to follow them; yet how often and how passionately, for a week, we came back together to the subject! Much as we had discussed it that Sunday night, I was, in the immediate later hours in especial—for it may be imagined whether I slept—still haunted with the shadow of something she had not told me. I myself had kept back nothing, but there was a word Mrs. Grose had kept back. I was sure, moreover, by morning, that this was not from a failure of frankness, but because on every side there were fears. It seems to me indeed, in retrospect, that by the time the morrow's sun was high I had restlessly read into the facts before us almost all the meaning they were to receive from subsequent and more cruel occurrences. What they gave me above all was just the sinister figure of the living man—the dead one would keep awhile!—and of the months he had continuously passed at Bly, which, added up, made a formidable stretch. The limit of this evil time had arrived only when, on the dawn of a winter's morning, Peter Quint was found, by a labourer going to early work, stone dead on the road from the village: a catastrophe explained—superficially at least—by a visible wound to his head; such a wound as might have been produced—and as, on the final evidence, *had* been—by a fatal slip, in the dark and after leaving the public house, on the steepish icy slope, a wrong path altogether, at the bottom of which he lay. The icy slope, the turn mistaken at night and in liquor, accounted for much—practically, in the end and after the inquest and boundless chatter, for everything; but there had been matters in his life—strange passages and perils, secret disorders, vices more than suspected—that would have accounted for a good deal more.

I scarce know how to put my story into words that shall be a credible picture of my state of mind; but I was in these days literally able to find a joy in the extraordinary flight of heroism the occasion demanded of me. I now saw that I had been asked for a service admirable and difficult; and there would be a greatness in letting it be seen—oh, in the right quarter!—that I could succeed where many another girl might have failed. It was an immense help to me—I confess I rather applaud myself as I look back!—that I saw my service so strongly and so simply. I was there to protect and defend the little crea-

tures in the world the most bereaved and the most love-able, the appeal of whose helplessness had suddenly become only too explicit, a deep, constant ache of one's own committed heart. We were cut off, really, together; we were united in our danger. They had nothing but me, and I—well, I had *them*. It was in short a magnificent chance. This chance presented itself to me in an image richly material. I was a screen—I was to stand before them. The more I saw, the less they would. I began to watch them in a stifled suspense, a disguised excitement that might well, had it continued too long, have turned to something like madness. What saved me, as I now see, was that it turned to something else altogether. It didn't last as suspense—it was superseded by horrible proofs. Proofs, I say, yes—from the moment I really took hold.

This moment dated from an afternoon hour that I happened to spend in the grounds with the younger of my pupils alone. We had left Miles indoors, on the red cushion of a deep window-seat; he had wished to finish a book, and I had been glad to encourage a purpose so laudable in a young man whose only defect was an occasional excess of the restless. His sister, on the contrary, had been alert to come out, and I strolled with her half an hour, seeking the shade, for the sun was still high and the day exceptionally warm. I was aware afresh, with her, as we went, of how, like her brother, she contrived—it was the charming thing in both children—to let me alone without appearing to drop me and to accompany me without appearing to surround. They were never importunate and yet never listless. My attention to them all really went to seeing them amuse themselves immensely without me: this was a spectacle they seemed actively to prepare and that engaged me as an active admirer. I walked in a world of their invention—they had no occasion whatever to draw upon mine; so that my time was taken only with being, for them, some remarkable person or thing that the game of the moment required and that was merely, thanks to my superior, my exalted stamp, a happy and highly distinguished sinecure. I forget what I was on the present occasion; I only remember that I was something very important and very quiet and that Flora was playing very hard. We were on the edge of the lake, and, as we had lately begun geography, the lake was the Sea of Azof.

Suddenly, in these circumstances, I became aware that, on the other side of the Sea of Azof, we had an interested spectator. The way this knowledge gathered in me was the strangest thing in the world—the strangest, that is, except the very much stranger in which it quickly merged itself. I had sat down with a piece of work—for I was something or other that could sit—on the old stone bench which overlooked the pond; and in this position I began to take in with certitude, and yet without direct vision, the presence, at a distance, of a third person. The old trees, the thick shrubbery, made a great and pleasant shade, but it was all suffused with the brightness of the hot, still hour. There was no ambiguity in anything; none whatever, at least, in the conviction I from one moment to another found myself forming as to what I should see straight before me and across the lake as a consequence of raising my eyes. They were attached at this juncture to the stitching in which I was engaged, and I can feel once more the spasm of my effort not to move them till I should so have steadied myself as to be able to make up my mind what to do. There was an alien object in view— a figure whose right of presence I instantly, passionately questioned. I recollect counting over perfectly the possibilities, reminding myself that nothing was more natural, for instance, than the appearance of one of the men about the place, or even of a messenger, a postman or a trades- man's boy, from the village. That reminder had as little effect on my practical certitude as I was conscious—still even without looking—of its having upon the character and attitude of our visitor. Nothing was more natural than that these things should be the other things that they absolutely were not.

Of the positive identity of the apparition I would assure myself as soon as the small clock of my courage should have ticked out the right second; meanwhile, with an effort that was already sharp enough, I transferred my eyes straight to little Flora, who, at the moment, was about ten yards away. My heart had stood still for an instant with the wonder and terror of the question whether she too would see; and I held my breath while I waited for what a cry from her, what some sudden innocent sign either of interest or of alarm, would tell me. I waited, but nothing came; then, in the first place—and there is something more dire in this, I feel, than in anything I have to relate—I was determined by a sense that, within a minute, all sounds from her had previously dropped; and, in the second, by the circumstance that, also within the minute, she had, in her play, turned her back to the water. This was her attitude when I at last looked at her—looked with the confirmed conviction that we were still, together, under direct personal notice. She had picked up a small flat piece of wood, which happened to have in it a little hole that had evidently suggested to her the idea of sticking in another fragment that might figure as a mast and make the thing a boat. This second morsel, as I watched her, she was very markedly and intently attempting to tighten in its place. My apprehension of what she was doing sustained me so that after some seconds I felt I was ready for more. Then I again shifted my eyes—I faced what I had to face.

VII

I GOT hold of Mrs. Grose as soon after this as I could; and I can give no intelligible account of how I fought out the interval. Yet I still hear myself cry as I fairly threw myself into her arms: "They *know*—it's too monstrous: they know, they know!"

"And what on earth——?" I felt her incredulity as she held me.

"Why, all that *we* know—and heaven knows what else besides!" Then, as she released me, I made it out to her, made it out perhaps only now with full coherency even to myself. "Two hours ago, in the garden"—I could scarce articulate—"Flora *saw!*"

Mrs. Grose took it as she might have taken a blow in the stomach. "She has told you?" she panted.

"Not a word—that's the horror. She kept it to herself! The child of eight, *that* child!" Unutterable still, for me, was the stupefaction of it.

Mrs. Grose, of course, could only gape the wider. "Then how do you know?"

"I was there—I saw with my eyes: saw that she was perfectly aware."

"Do you mean aware of *him?*"

"No—of *her*." I was conscious as I spoke that I looked prodigious things, for I got the slow reflection of them in my companion's face. "Another person—this time; but a figure of quite as unmistakeable horror and evil: a woman in black, pale and dreadful—with such an air also, and such a face!—on the other side of the lake. I was there with the child—quiet for the hour; and in the midst of it she came."

"Came how—from where?"

"From where they come from! She just appeared and stood there—but not so near."

"And without coming nearer?"

"Oh, for the effect and the feeling, she might have been as close as you!"

My friend, with an odd impulse, fell back a step. "Was she someone you've never seen?"

"Yes. But someone the child has. Someone *you* have." Then, to show how I had thought it all out: "My predecessor—the one who died."

"Miss Jessel?"

"Miss Jessel. You don't believe me?" I pressed.

She turned right and left in her distress. "How can you be sure?"

This drew from me, in the state of my nerves, a flash of impatience. "Then ask Flora—*she's* sure!" But I had no sooner spoken than I caught myself up. "No, for God's sake, *don't!* She'll say she isn't—she'll lie!"

Mrs. Grose was not too bewildered instinctively to protest. "Ah, how *can* you?"

"Because I'm clear. Flora doesn't want me to know."

"It's only then to spare you."

"No, no—there are depths, depths! The more I go over it, the more I see in it, and the more I see in it the more I fear. I don't know what I *don't* see—what I *don't* fear!"

Mrs. Grose tried to keep up with me. "You mean you're afraid of seeing her again?"

"Oh, no; that's nothing—now!" Then I explained. "It's of *not* seeing her."

But my companion only looked wan. "I don't understand you."

"Why, it's that the child may keep it up—and that the child assuredly *will*—without my knowing it."

At the image of this possibility Mrs. Grose for a moment collapsed, yet presently to pull herself together again, as if from the positive force of the sense of what, should we yield an inch, there would really be to give way to. "Dear, dear—we must keep our heads! And after all, if she doesn't mind it——!" She even tried a grim joke. "Perhaps she likes it!"

"Likes *such* things—a scrap of an infant!"

"Isn't it just a proof of her blessed innocence?" my friend bravely inquired.

She brought me, for the instant, almost round. "Oh, we must clutch at *that*—we must cling to it! If it isn't a proof of what you say, it's a proof of—God knows what! For the woman's a horror of horrors."

Mrs. Grose, at this, fixed her eyes a minute on the ground; then at last raising them, "Tell me how you know," she said.

"Then you admit it's what she was?" I cried.

"Tell me how you know," my friend simply repeated.

"Know? By seeing her! By the way she looked."

"At you, do you mean—so wickedly?"

"Dear me, no—I could have borne that. She gave me never a glance. She only fixed the child."

Mrs. Grose tried to see it. "Fixed her?"

"Ah, with such awful eyes!"

She stared at mine as if they might really have resembled them. "Do you mean of dislike?"

"God help us, no. Of something much worse."

"Worse than dislike?"—this left her indeed at a loss.

"With a determination—indescribable. With a kind of fury of intention."

I made her turn pale. "Intention?"

"To get hold of her." Mrs. Grose—her eyes just lingering on mine—gave a shudder and walked to the window; and while she stood there looking out I completed my statement. "*That's* what Flora knows."

After a little she turned round. "The person was in black, you say?"

"In mourning—rather poor, almost shabby. But—yes —with extraordinary beauty." I now recognised to what I had at last, stroke by stroke, brought the victim of my confidence, for she quite visibly weighed this. "Oh, handsome—very, very," I insisted; "wonderfully handsome. But infamous."

She slowly came back to me. "Miss Jessel—*was* infamous." She once more took my hand in both her own, holding it as tight as if to fortify me against the increase of alarm I might draw from this disclosure. "They were both infamous," she finally said.

So, for a little, we faced it once more together; and I found absolutely a degree of help in seeing it now so straight. "I appreciate," I said, "the great decency of your not having hitherto spoken; but the time has certainly come to give me the whole thing." She appeared to assent to this, but still only in silence; seeing which I went on: "I must have it now. Of what did she die? Come, there was something between them."

"There was everything."

"In spite of the difference——?"

"Oh, of their rank, their condition"—she brought it woefully out. "*She* was a lady."

I turned it over; I again saw. "Yes—she was a lady."

"And he so dreadfully below," said Mrs. Grose.

I felt that I doubtless needn't press too hard, in such company, on the place of a servant in the scale; but there was nothing to prevent an acceptance of my companion's own measure of my predecessor's abasement. There was a way to deal with that, and I dealt; the more readily for my full vision—on the evidence—of our employer's late clever, good-looking "own" man; impudent, assured, spoiled, depraved. "The fellow was a hound."

Mrs. Grose considered as if it were perhaps a little a case for a sense of shades. "I've never seen one like him. He did what he wished."

"With *her?*"

"With them all."

It was as if now in my friend's own eyes Miss Jessel had again appeared. I seemed at any rate, for an instant, to see their evocation of her as distinctly as I had seen her by the pond; and I brought out with decision: "It must have been also what *she* wished!"

Mrs. Grose's face signified that it had been indeed, but she said at the same time: "Poor woman—she paid for it!"

"Then you do know what she died of?" I asked.

"No—I know nothing. I wanted not to know; I was glad enough I didn't; and I thanked heaven she was well out of this!"

"Yet you had, then, your idea——"

"Of her real reason for leaving? Oh, yes—as to that. She couldn't have stayed. Fancy it here—for a governess! And afterwards I imagined—and I still imagine. And what I imagine is dreadful."

"Not so dreadful as what *I* do," I replied; on which I must have shown her—as I was indeed but too conscious —a front of miserable defeat. It brought out again all her compassion for me, and at the renewed touch of her kindness my power to resist broke down. I burst, as I had, the other time, made her burst, into tears; she took me to her motherly breast, and my lamentation overflowed. "I don't do it!" I sobbed in despair; "I don't save or shield them! It's far worse than I dreamed—they're lost!"

VIII

WHAT I had said to Mrs. Grose was true enough: there were in the matter I had put before her depths and possibilities that I lacked resolution to sound; so that when we met once more in the wonder of it we were of a common mind about the duty of resistance to extravagant fancies. We were to keep our heads if we should keep nothing else —difficult indeed as that might be in the face of what, in our prodigious experience, was least to be questioned. Late that night, while the house slept, we had another talk in my room, when she went all the way with me as to its being beyond doubt that I had seen exactly what I had seen. To hold her perfectly in the pinch of that, I found I had only to ask her how, if I had "made it up," I came to be able to give, of each of the persons appearing to me, a picture disclosing, to the last detail, their special marks—a portrait on the exhibition of which she had instantly recognised and named them. She wished, of course,—small blame to her!—to sink the whole subject; and I was quick to assure her that my own interest in it had now violently taken the form of a search for the way to escape from it. I encountered her on the ground of a probability that with recurrence—for recurrence we took for granted—I should get used to my danger, distinctly professing that my personal exposure had suddenly become the least of my discomforts. It was my new suspicion that was intolerable; and yet even to this complication the later hours of the day had brought a little ease.

On leaving her, after my first outbreak, I had of course returned to my pupils, associating the right remedy for my dismay with that sense of their charm which I had already found to be a thing I could positively cultivate and which had never failed me yet. I had simply, in other words, plunged afresh into Flora's special society and there become aware—it was almost a luxury!—that she could put her little conscious hand straight upon the spot that ached. She had looked at me in sweet speculation and then had accused me to my face of having "cried." I had supposed I had brushed away the ugly signs: but I could literally—for the time, at all events—rejoice, under this fathomless charity, that they had not entirely disappeared. To gaze into the depths of blue of the child's eyes and pronounce their loveliness a trick of premature cunning was to be guilty of a cynicism in preference to which I naturally preferred to abjure my judgment and, so far as might be, my agitation. I couldn't adjure for merely wanting to, but I could repeat to Mrs. Grose—as I did there, over and over, in the small hours—that with their voices in the air, their pressure on one's heart and their fragrant faces against one's cheek, everything fell to the ground but their incapacity and their beauty. It was a pity that, somehow, to settle this once for all, I had equally to re-enumerate the signs of subtlety that, in the afternoon, by the lake, had made a miracle of my show of self-possession. It was a pity to be obliged to re-investigate the certitude of the moment itself and repeat how it had come to me as a revelation that the inconceivable communion I then surprised was a matter, for either party, of habit. It was a pity that I should have had to quaver out again the reasons for my not having, in my delusion, so much as questioned that the little girl saw our visitant even as I actually saw Mrs. Grose herself, and that she wanted, by just so much as she did thus see, to make me suppose she didn't, and at the same time, without showing anything, arrive at a guess as to whether I myself did! It was a pity that I needed once more to describe the portentous little activity by which she sought to divert my attention—the perceptible increase of move-

ment, the greater intensity of play, the singing, the gab-
bling of nonsense, and the invitation to romp.

Yet if I had not indulged, to prove there was nothing in
it, in this review, I should have missed the two or three
dim elements of comfort that still remained to me. I
should not for instance have been able to asseverate to
my friend that I was certain—which was so much to the
good—that *I* at least had not betrayed myself. I should
not have been prompted, by stress of need, by desperation
of mind,—I scarce know what to call it,—to invoke such
further aid to intelligence as might spring from pushing
my colleague fairly to the wall. She had told me, bit by
bit, under pressure, a great deal; but a small shifty spot
on the wrong side of it all still sometimes brushed my
brow like the wing of a bat; and I remember how on this
occasion—for the sleeping house and the concentration
alike of our danger and our watch seemed to help—I felt
the importance of giving the last jerk to the curtain. "I
don't believe anything so horrible," I recollect saying;
"no, let us put it definitely, my dear, that I don't. But if
I did, you know, there's a thing I should require now,
just without sparing you the least bit more—oh, not a
scrap, come!—to get out of you. What was it you had in
mind when, in our distress, before Miles came back, over
the letter from his school, you said, under my insistence,
that you didn't pretend for him that he had not literally
ever been 'bad'? He has *not* literally 'ever,' in these weeks
that I myself have lived with him and so closely watched
him; he has been an imperturbable little prodigy of delightful, loveable goodness. Therefore you might perfectly have made the claim for him if you had not, as it
happened, seen an exception to take. What was your exception, and to what passage in your personal observation
of him did you refer?"

It was a dreadfully austere inquiry, but levity was not
our note, and, at any rate, before the grey dawn admonished us to separate I had got my answer. What my friend

had had in mind proved to be immensely to the purpose. It was neither more nor less than the circumstance that for a period of several months Quint and the boy had been perpetually together. It was in fact the very appropriate truth that she had ventured to criticise the propriety, to hint at the incongruity, of so close an alliance, and even to go so far on the subject as a frank overture to Miss Jessel. Miss Jessel had, with a most strange manner, requested her to mind her business, and the good woman had, on this, directly approached little Miles. What she had said to him, since I pressed, was that *she* liked to see young gentlemen not forget their station.

I pressed again, of course, at this. "You reminded him that Quint was only a base menial?"

"As you might say! And it was his answer, for one thing, that was bad."

"And for another thing?" I waited. "He repeated your words to Quint?"

"No, not that. It's just what he *wouldn't!*" she could still impress upon me. "I was sure, at any rate," she added, "that he didn't. But he denied certain occasions."

"What occasions?"

"When they had been about together quite as if Quint were his tutor—and a very grand one—and Miss Jessel only for the little lady. When he had gone off with the fellow, I mean, and spent hours with him."

"He then prevaricated about it—he said he hadn't?" Her assent was clear enough to cause me to add in a moment: "I see. He lied."

"Oh!" Mrs. Grose mumbled. This was a suggestion that it didn't matter; which indeed she backed up by a further remark. "You see, after all, Miss Jessel didn't mind. She didn't forbid him."

I considered. "Did he put that to you as a justification?"

At this she dropped again. "No, he never spoke of it."

"Never mentioned her in connection with Quint?"

She saw, visibly flushing, where I was coming out. "Well, he didn't show anything. He denied," she repeated; "he denied."

Lord, how I pressed her now! "So that you could see he knew what was between the two wretches?"

"I don't know—I don't know!" the poor woman groaned.

"You do know, you dear thing," I replied; "only you haven't my dreadful boldness of mind, and you keep back, out of timidity and modesty and delicacy, even the impression that, in the past, when you had, without my aid, to flounder about in silence, most of all made you miserable. But I shall get it out of you yet! There was something in the boy that suggested to you," I continued, "that he covered and concealed their relation."

"Oh, he couldn't prevent——"

"Your learning the truth? I dare say! But, heavens," I fell, with vehemence, a-thinking, "what it shows that they must, to that extent, have succeeded in making of him!"

"Ah nothing that's not nice *now*!" Mrs. Grose lugubriously pleaded.

"I don't wonder you looked queer," I persisted, "when I mentioned to you the letter from his school!"

"I doubt if I looked as queer as you!" she retorted with homely force. "And if he was so bad then as that comes to, how is he such an angel now?"

"Yes, indeed—and if he was a fiend at school! How, how, how? Well," I said in my torment, "you must put it to me again, but I shall not be able to tell you for some days. Only, put it to me again!" I cried in a way that made my friend stare. "There are directions in which I must not for the present let myself go." Meanwhile I returned to her first example—the one to which she had just previously referred—of the boy's happy capacity for an occasional slip. "If Quint—on your remonstrance at the time you speak of—was a base menial, one of the things Miles said to you. I find myself guessing. was that you

were another." Again her admission was so adequate that
I continued: "And you forgave him that?"

"Wouldn't *you*?"

"Oh, yes!" And we exchanged there, in the stillness, a
sound of the oddest amusement. Then I went on: "At all
events, while he was with the man——"

"Miss Flora was with the woman. It suited them all!"

It suited me too, I felt, only too well; by which I mean
that it suited exactly the particularly deadly view I was
in the very act of forbidding myself to entertain. But I
so far succeeded in checking the expression of this view
that I will throw, just here, no further light on it than
may be offered by the mention of my final observation
to Mrs. Grose. "His having lied and been impudent are,
I confess, less engaging specimens than I had hoped to
have from you of the outbreak in him of the little natural
man. Still," I mused, "they must do, for they make me
feel more than ever that I must watch."

It made me blush, the next minute, to see in my friend's
face how much more unreservedly she had forgiven him
than her anecdote struck me as presenting to my own
tenderness an occasion for doing. This came out when,
at the schoolroom door, she quitted me. "Surely you don't
accuse *him*——"

"Of carrying on an intercourse that he conceals from
me? Ah, remember that, until further evidence, I now
accuse nobody." Then, before shutting her out to go, by
another passage, to her own place, "I must just wait," I
wound up.

IX

I WAITED and waited, and the days, as they elapsed, took something from my consternation. A very few of them, in fact, passing, in constant sight of my pupils, without a fresh incident, sufficed to give to grievous fancies and even to odious memories a kind of brush of the sponge. I have spoken of the surrender to their extraordinary childish grace as a thing I could actively cultivate, and it may be imagined if I neglected now to address myself to this source for whatever it would yield. Stranger than I can express, certainly, was the effort to struggle against my new lights; it would doubtless have been, however, a greater tension still had it not been so frequently successful. I used to wonder how my little charges could help guessing that I thought strange things about them; and the circumstance that these things only made them more interesting was not by itself a direct aid to keeping them in the dark. I trembled lest they should see that they *were* so immensely more interesting. Putting things at the worst, at all events, as in meditation I so often did, any clouding of their innocence could only be—blameless and foredoomed as they were—a reason the more for taking risks. There were moments when, by an irresistible impulse, I found myself catching them up and pressing them to my heart. As soon as I had done so I used to say to myself: "What will they think of that? Doesn't it betray too much?" It would have been easy to get into a sad, wild tangle about how much I might betray; but the real account, I feel, of the hours of peace that I could still enjoy was that the immediate charm of my companions was a beguilement still effective even under the shadow of the possibility that it was studied.

For if it occurred to me that I might occasionally excite suspicion by the little outbreaks of my sharper passion for them, so too I remember wondering if I mightn't see a queerness in the traceable increase of their own demonstrations.

They were at this period extravagantly and preternaturally fond of me; which, after all, I could reflect, was no more than a graceful response in children perpetually bowed over and hugged. The homage of which they were so lavish succeeded, in truth, for my nerves, quite as well as if I never appeared to myself, as I may say, literally to catch them at a purpose in it. They had never, I think, wanted to do so many things for their poor protectress; I mean—though they got their lessons better and better, which was naturally what would please her most—in the way of diverting, entertaining, surprising her; reading her passages, telling her stories, acting her charades, pouncing out at her, in disguises, as animals and historical characters, and above all astonishing her by the "pieces" they had secretly got by heart and could interminably recite. I should never get to the bottom— were I to let myself go even now—of the prodigious private commentary, all under still more private correction, with which, in these days, I overscored their full hours. They had shown me from the first a facility for everything, a general faculty which, taking a fresh start, achieved remarkable flights. They got their little tasks as if they loved them, and indulged, from the mere exuberance of the gift, in the most unimposed little miracles of memory. They not only popped out at me as tigers and as Romans, but as Shakespeareans, astronomers, and navigators. This was so singularly the case that it had presumably much to do with the fact as to which, at the present day, I am at a loss for a different explanation: I allude to my unnatural composure on the subject of another school for Miles. What I remember is that I was content not, for the time, to open the question, and that

contentment must have sprung from the sense of his perpetually striking show of cleverness. He was too clever
for a bad governess, for a parson's daughter, to spoil; and
the strangest if not the brightest thread in the pensive
embroidery I just spoke of was the impression I might
have got, if I had dared to work it out, that he was under
some influence operating in his small intellectual life as a
tremendous incitement.

If it was easy to reflect, however, that such a boy
could postpone school, it was at least as marked that for
such a boy to have been "kicked out" by a school-master
was a mystification without end. Let me add that in their
company now—and I was careful almost never to be out
of it—I could follow no scent very far. We lived in a
cloud of music and love and success and private theatri-
cals. The musical sense in each of the children was of the
quickest, but the elder in especial had a marvellous knack
of catching and repeating. The schoolroom piano broke
into all gruesome fancies; and when that failed there were
confabulations in corners, with a sequel of one of them
going out in the highest spirits in order to "come in" as
something new. I had had brothers myself, and it was no
revelation to me that little girls could be slavish idolaters
of little boys. What surpassed everything was that there
was a little boy in the world who could have for the in-
ferior age, sex, and intelligence so fine a consideration.
They were extraordinarily at one, and to say that they
never either quarrelled or complained is to make the note
of praise coarse for their quality of sweetness. Sometimes,
indeed, when I dropped into coarseness, I perhaps came
across traces of little understandings between them by
which one of them should keep me occupied while the
other slipped away. There is a *naïf* side, I suppose, in all
diplomacy; but if my pupils practised upon me, it was
surely with the minimum of grossness. It was all in the
other quarter that, after a lull, the grossness broke out.

I find that I really hang back; but I must take my

plunge. In going on with the record of what was hideous
at Bly, I not only challenge the most liberal faith—for
which I little care; but—and this is another matter—I
renew what I myself suffered, I again push my way
through it to the end. There came suddenly an hour after
which, as I look back, the affair seems to me to have been
all pure suffering; but I have at least reached the heart
of it, and the straightest road out is doubtless to advance.
One evening—with nothing to lead up or to prepare it—I
felt the cold touch of the impression that had breathed
on me the night of my arrival and which, much lighter
then, as I have mentioned, I should probably have made
little of in memory had my subsequent sojourn been less
agitated. I had not gone to bed; I sat reading by a couple
of candles. There was a roomful of old books at Bly—last-
century fiction, some of it, which, to the extent of a distinctly deprecated renown, but never to so much as that
of a stray specimen, had reached the sequestered home
and appealed to the unavowed curiosity of my youth. I
remember that the book I had in my hand was Fielding's
Amelia; also that I was wholly awake. I recall further
both a general conviction that it was horribly late and a
particular objection to looking at my watch. I figure,
finally, that the white curtain draping, in the fashion of
those days, the head of Flora's little bed, shrouded, as I
had assured myself long before, the perfection of childish
rest. I recollect in short that, though I was deeply interested in my author, I found myself, at the turn of a page
and with his spell all scattered, looking straight up from
him and hard at the door of my room. There was a moment during which I listened, reminded of the faint sense
I had had, the first night, of there being something unde-
fineably astir in the house, and noted the soft breath of
the open casement just move the half-drawn blind. Then,
with all the marks of a deliberation that must have
seemed magnificent had there been anyone to admire it, I
laid down my book, rose to my feet, and, taking a candle,

went straight out of the room and, from the passage, on which my light made little impression, noiselessly closed and locked the door.

I can say now neither what determined nor what guided me, but I went straight along the lobby, holding my candle high, till I came within sight of the tall window that presided over the great turn of the staircase. At this point I precipitately found myself aware of three things. They were practically simultaneous, yet they had flashes of succession. My candle, under a bold flourish, went out, and I perceived, by the uncovered window, that the yielding dusk of earliest morning rendered it unnecessary. Without it, the next instant, I saw that there was some-one on the stair. I speak of sequences, but I required no lapse of seconds to stiffen myself for a third encounter with Quint. The apparition had reached the landing half-way up and was therefore on the spot nearest the window, where at sight of me, it stopped short and fixed me exactly as it had fixed me from the tower and from the garden. He knew me as well as I knew him; and so, in the cold, faint twilight, with a glimmer in the high glass and another on the polish of the oak stair below, we faced each other in our common intensity. He was absolutely, on this occasion, a living, detestable, dangerous presence. But that was not the wonder of wonders; I reserve this distinction for quite another circumstance: the circumstance that dread had unmistakeably quitted me and that there was nothing in me there that didn't meet and measure him.

I had plenty of anguish after that extraordinary moment, but I had, thank God, no terror. And he knew I had not—I found myself at the end of an instant magnificently aware of this. I felt, in a fierce rigour of confidence, that if I stood my ground a minute I should cease—for the time, at least—to have him to reckon with; and during the minute, accordingly, the thing was as human and hideous as a real interview: hideous just because it *was* human, as human as to have met alone, in the small hours, in a sleeping house, some enemy, some adventurer, some criminal. It was the dead silence of our long gaze at such close quarters that gave the whole horror, huge as it was, its only note of the unnatural. If I had met a murderer in such a place and at such an hour, we still at least would have spoken. Something would have passed, in life, between us; if nothing had passed one of us would have moved. The moment was so prolonged that it would have taken but little more to make me doubt if even *I* were in life. I can't express what followed it save by saying that the silence itself—which was indeed in a manner an attestation of my strength—became the element into which I saw the figure disappear; in which I definitely saw it turn as I might have seen the low wretch to which it had once belonged turn on receipt of an order, and pass, with my eyes on the villainous back that no hunch could have more disfigured, straight down the staircase and into the darkness in which the next bend was lost.

X

I REMAINED awhile at the top of the stair, but with the effect presently of understanding that when my visitor had gone, he had gone: then I returned to my room. The foremost thing I saw there by the light of the candle I had left burning was that Flora's little bed was empty; and on this I caught my breath with all the terror that, five minutes before, I had been able to resist. I dashed at the place in which I had left her lying and over which (for the small silk counterpane and the sheets were disarranged) the white curtains had been deceivingly pulled forward; then my step, to my unutterable relief, produced an answering sound: I perceived an agitation of the window-blind, and the child, ducking down, emerged rosily from the other side of it. She stood there in so much of her candour and so little of her nightgown, with her pink bare feet and the golden glow of her curls. She looked intensely grave, and I had never had such a sense of losing an advantage acquired (the thrill of which had just been so prodigious) as on my consciousness that she addressed me with a reproach. "You naughty: where *have* you been?"—instead of challenging her own irregularity I found myself arraigned and explaining. She herself explained, for that matter, with the loveliest, eagerest simplicity. She had known suddenly, as she lay there, that I was out of the room, and had jumped up to see what had become of me. I had dropped, with the joy of her reappearance, back into my chair—feeling then, and then only, a little faint; and she had pattered straight over to me, thrown herself upon my knee, given herself to be held with the flame of the candle full in the wonderful little face that was still flushed with sleep. I remember closing my eyes an instant, yieldingly, consciously, as before the excess of something beautiful that shone out of the blue of her own. "You were looking for me out of the window?" I said. "You thought I might be walking in the grounds?"

"Well, you know, I thought someone was"—she never blanched as she smiled out that at me.

Oh, how I looked at her now! "And did you see anyone?"

"Ah, *no!*" she returned, almost with the full privilege of childish inconsequence, resentfully, though with a long sweetness in her little drawl of the negative.

At that moment, in the state of my nerves, I absolutely believed she lied; and if I once more closed my eyes it was before the dazzle of the three or four possible ways in which I might take this up. One of these, for a moment, tempted me with such singular intensity that, to withstand it, I must have gripped my little girl with a spasm that, wonderfully, she submitted to without a cry or a sign of fright. Why not break out at her on the spot and have it all over?—give it to her straight in her lovely little lighted face? "You see, you see, you *know* that you do and that you already quite suspect I believe it; therefore why not frankly confess it to me, so that we may at least live with it together and learn perhaps, in the strangeness of our fate, where we are and what it means?" This solicitation dropped, alas, as it came: if I could immediately have succumbed to it I might have spared myself——well you'll see what. Instead of succumbing I sprang again to my feet, looked at her bed, and took a helpless middle way. "Why did you pull the curtain over the place to make me think you were still there?"

Flora luminously considered; after which, with her little divine smile: "Because I don't like to frighten you!"

"But if I had, by your idea, gone out——?"

She absolutely declined to be puzzled; she turned her eyes to the flame of the candle as if the question were as irrelevant, or at any rate as impersonal, as Mrs. Marcet or nine-times-nine. "Oh, but you know," she quite adequately answered, "that you might come back, you dear, and that you *have!*" And after a little, when she had got into bed, I had, for a long time, by almost sitting on her to hold her hand, to prove that I recognised the pertinence of my return.

You may imagine the general complexion, from that moment, of my nights. I repeatedly sat up till I didn't know when; I selected moments when my room-mate unmistakeably slept, and, stealing out, took noiseless turns in the passage and even pushed as far as to where I had last met Quint. But I never met him there again; and I may as well say at once that I on no other occasion saw him in the house. I just missed, on the staircase, on the other hand, a different adventure. Looking down it from the top I once recognised the presence of a woman seated on one of the lower steps with her back presented to me, her body half bowed and her head, in an attiutde of woe, in her hands. I had been there but an instant, however, when she vanished without looking round at me. I knew, none the less, exactly what dreadful face she had to show; and I wondered whether, if instead of being above I had been below, I should have had, for going up, the same nerve I had lately shown Quint. Well, there continued to be plenty of chance for nerve. On the eleventh night after my latest encounter with that gentleman—they were all numbered now—I had an alarm that perilously skirted it and that indeed, from the particular quality of its unexpectedness, proved quite my sharpest shock. It was precisely the first night during this series that, weary with watching, I had felt that I might again without laxity lay myself down at my old hour. I slept immediately and, as I afterwards know, till about one o'clock; but when I woke it was to sit straight up, as completely roused as if a hand had shook me. I had left a light burning, but it was now out, and I felt an instant certainty that Flora had extinguished it. This brought me to my feet and straight, in the darkness, to her bed, which I found she had left. A glance at the window enlightened me further, and the striking of a match completed the picture.

The child had again got up—this time blowing out the taper, and had again, for some purpose of observation or response, squeezed in behind the blind and was peering out into the night. That she now saw—as she had not, I had satisfied myself, the previous time—was proved to me by the fact that she was disturbed neither by my re-illumination nor by the haste I made to get into slippers and into a wrap. Hidden, protected, absorbed, she evidently rested on the sill—the casement opened forward—and gave herself up. There was a great still moon to help her, and this fact had counted in my quick decision. She was face to face with the apparition we had met at the lake, and could not communicate with it as she had not then been able to do. What I, on my side, had to care for was, without disturbing her, to reach, from the corridor, some other window in the same quarter. I got to the door without her hearing me; I got out of it, closed it and listened, from the other side, for some sound from her. While I stood in the passage I had my eyes on her brother's door, which was but ten steps off and which, indescribably, produced in me a renewal of the strange impulse that I lately spoke of as my temptation. What if I should go straight in and march to *his* window?—what if, by risking to his boyish bewilderment a revelation of my motive, I should throw across the rest of the mystery the long halter of my boldness?

This thought held me sufficiently to make me cross to his threshold and pause again. I preternaturally listened; I figured to myself what might portentously be; I wondered if his bed were also empty and he too were secretly at watch. It was a deep, soundless minute, at the end of which my impulse failed. He was quiet; he might be innocent; the risk was hideous; I turned away. There was a figure in the grounds—a figure prowling for a sight, the visitor with whom Flora was engaged; but it was not the visitor most concerned with my boy. I hesitated afresh, but on other grounds and only a few seconds; then I had made my choice. There were empty rooms at Bly, and it was only a question of choosing the right one. The right one suddenly presented itself to me as the lower one—though high above the gardens—in the solid corner of the house that I have spoken of as the old tower. This was a large, square chamber, arranged with some state as a bedroom, the extravagant size of which made it so inconvenient that it had not for years, though kept by Mrs. Grose in exemplary order, been occupied. I had often admired it and I knew my way about in it; I had only, after just faltering at the first chill gloom of its disuse, to pass across it and unbolt as quietly as I could one of the shutters. Achieving this transit, I uncovered the glass without a sound and, applying my face to the pane, was able, the darkness without being much less than within, to see that I commanded the right direction. Then I saw something more. The moon made the night extraordinarily penetrable and showed me on the lawn a person, diminished by distance, who stood there motionless and as if fascinated, looking up to where I had appeared—looking, that is, not so much straight at me as at something that was apparently above me. There was clearly another person above me—there was a person on the tower; but the presence on the lawn was not in the least what I had conceived and had confidently hurried to meet. The presence on the lawn—I felt sick as I made it out—was poor little Miles himself.

XI

It was not till late next day that I spoke to Mrs. Grose; the rigour with which I kept my pupils in sight making it often difficult to meet her privately, and the more as we each felt the importance of not provoking—on the part of the servants quite as much as on that of the children— any suspicion of a secret flurry or of a discussion of mysteries. I drew a great security in this particular from her mere smooth aspect. There was nothing in her fresh face to pass on to others my horrible confidences. She believed me, I was sure, absolutely: if she hadn't I don't know what would have become of me, for I couldn't have borne the business alone. But she was a magnificent monument to the blessing of a want of imagination, and if she could see in our little charges nothing but their beauty and amiability, their happiness and cleverness, she had no direct communication with the sources of my trouble. If they had been at all visibly blighted or battered, she would doubtless have grown, on tracing it back, haggard enough to match them; as matters stood, however, I could feel her, when she surveyed them, with her large white arms folded and the habit of serenity in all her look, thank the Lord's mercy that if they were ruined the pieces would still serve. Flights of fancy gave place, in her mind, to a steady fireside glow, and I had already begun to perceive how, with the development of the conviction that —as time went on without a public accident—our young things could, after all, look out for themselves, she addressed her greatest solicitude to the sad case presented by their instructress. That, for myself, was a sound simplification: I could engage that, to the world, my face should tell no tales, but it would have been, in the conditions, an immense added strain to find myself anxious about hers.

At the hour I now speak of she had joined me, under pressure, on the terrace, where, with the lapse of the season, the afternoon sun was now agreeable; and we sat there together while, before us, at a distance, but within call if we wished, the children strolled to and fro in one of their most manageable moods. They moved slowly, in unison, below us, over the lawn, the boy, as they went, reading aloud from a story-book and passing his arm round his sister to keep her quite in touch. Mrs. Grose watched them with positive placidity; then I caught the suppressed intellectual creak with which she conscientiously turned to take from me a view of the back of the tapestry. I had made her a receptacle of lurid things, but there was an odd recognition of my superiority—my accomplishments and my function—in her patience under my pain. She offered her mind to my disclosures as, had I wished to mix a witch's broth and proposed it with assurance, she would have held out a large clean saucepan. This had become thoroughly her attitude by the time that, in my recital of the events of the night, I reached the point of what Miles had said to me when, after seeing him, at such a monstrous hour, almost on the very spot where he happened now to be, I had gone down to bring him in; choosing then, at the window, with a concentrated need of not alarming the house, rather that method than a signal more resonant. I had left her meanwhile in little doubt of my small hope of representing with success even to her actual sympathy my sense of the real splendour of the little inspiration with which, after I had got him into the house, the boy met my final articulate challenge. As soon as I appeared in the moonlight on the terrace, he had come to me as straight as possible; on which I had taken his hand without a word and led him, through the dark spaces, up the staircase where Quint had so hungrily hovered for him, along the lobby where I had listened and trembled, and so to his forsaken room.

Not a sound, on the way, had passed between us, and I had wondered—oh, *how* I had wondered!—if he were groping about in his little mind for something plausible and not too grotesque. It would tax his invention, certainly, and I felt, this time, over his real embarrassment, a curious thrill of triumph. It was a sharp trap for the inscrutable! He couldn't play any longer at innocence; so how the deuce would he get out of it? There beat in me indeed, with the passionate throb of this question, an equal dumb appeal as to how the deuce *I* should. I was confronted at last, as never yet, with all the risk attached even now to sounding my own horrid note. I remember in fact that as we pushed into his little chamber, where the bed had not been slept in at all and the window, uncovered to the moonlight, made the place so clear that there was no need of striking a match—I remember how I suddenly dropped, sank upon the edge of the bed from the force of the idea that he must know how he really, as they say, "had" me. He could do what he liked, with all his cleverness to help him, so long as I should continue to defer to the old tradition of the criminality of those caretakers of the young who minister to superstitions and fears. He "had" me indeed, and in a cleft stick; for who would ever absolve me, who would consent that I should go unhung, if, by the faintest tremor of an overture, I were the first to introduce into our perfect intercourse an element so dire? No, no: it was useless to attempt to convey to Mrs. Grose, just as it is scarcely less so to attempt to suggest here, how, in our short, stiff brush in the dark, he fairly shook me with admiration. I was of course thoroughly kind and merciful; never, never yet had I placed on his little shoulders hands of such tenderness as those with which, while I rested against the bed, I held him there well under fire. I had no alternative but, in form at least, to put it to him.

"You must tell me now—and all the truth. What did you go out for? What were you doing there?"

I can still see his wonderful smile, the whites of his beautiful eyes, and the uncovering of his little teeth shine to me in the dusk. "If I tell you why, will you understand?" My heart, at this, leaped into my mouth. *Would* he tell me why? I found no sound on my lips to press it, and I was aware of replying only with a vague, repeated, grimacing nod. He was gentleness itself, and while I wagged my head at him he stood there more than ever a little fairy prince. It was his brightness indeed that gave me a respite. Would it be so great if he were really going to tell me? "Well," he said at last, "just exactly in order that you should do this."

"Do what?"

"Think me—for a change—*bad!*" I shall never forget the sweetness and gaiety with which he brought out the word, nor how, on top of it, he bent forward and kissed me. It was practically the end of everything. I met his kiss and I had to make, while I folded him for a minute in my arms, the most stupendous effort not to cry. He had given exactly the account of himself that permitted least of my going behind it, and it was only with the effect of confirming my acceptance of it that, as I presently glanced about the room, I could say—

"Then you didn't undress at all?"

He fairly glittered in the gloom. "Not at all. I sat up and read."

"And when did you go down?"

"At midnight. When I'm bad I *am* bad!"

"I see, I see—it's charming. But how could you be sure I would know it?"

"Oh, I arranged that with Flora." His answers rang out with a readiness! "She was to get up and look out."

"Which is what she did do." It was I who fell into the trap!

"So she disturbed you, and, to see what she was looking at, you also looked—you saw."

"While you," I concurred, "caught your death in the night air!"

He literally bloomed so from this exploit that he could afford radiantly to assent. "How otherwise should I have been bad enough?" he asked. Then, after another embrace, the incident and our interview closed on my recognition of all the reserves of goodness that, for his joke, he had been able to draw upon.

XII

THE particular impression I had received proved in the morning light, I repeat, not quite successfully presentable to Mrs. Grose, though I reinforced it with the mention of still another remark that he had made before we separated. "It all lies in half-a-dozen words," I said to her, "words that really settle the matter. 'Think, you know, what I *might* do!' He threw that off to show me how good he is. He knows down to the ground what he 'might' do. That's what he gave them a taste of at school."

"Lord, you do change!" cried my friend.

"I don't change—I simply make it out. The four, depend upon it, perpetually meet. If on either of these last nights you had been with either child, you would clearly have understood. The more I've watched and waited the more I've felt that if there were nothing else to make it sure it would be made so by the systematic silence of each. *Never*, by a slip of the tongue, have they so much as alluded to either of their old friends, any more than Miles has alluded to his expulsion. Oh yes, we may sit here and look at them, and they may show off to us there to their fill; but even while they pretend to be lost in their fairy-tale they're steeped in their vision of the dead restored. He's not reading to her," I declared; "they're talking of *them*—they're talking horrors! I go on, I know, as if I were crazy; and it's a wonder I'm not. What I've seen would have made *you* so; but it has only made me more lucid, made me get hold of still other things."

My lucidity must have seemed awful, but the charming creatures who were victims of it, passing and repassing in their interlocked sweetness, gave my colleague something to hold on by; and I felt how tight she held

72

as, without stirring in the breath of my passion, she covered them still with her eyes. "Of what other things have you got hold?"

"Why, of the very things that have delighted, fascinated, and yet, at bottom, as I now so strangely see, mystified and troubled me. Their more than earthly beauty, their absolutely unnatural goodness. It's a game," I went one; "it's a policy and a fraud!"

"On the part of little darlings——?"

"As yet mere lovely babies? Yes, mad as that seems!" The very act of bringing it out really helped me to trace it—follow it all up and piece it all together. "They haven't been good—they've only been absent. It has been easy to live with them, because they're simply leading a life of their own. They're not mine—they're not ours. They're his and they're hers!"

"Quint's and that woman's?"

"Quint's and that woman's. They want to get to them."

Oh, how, at this, poor Mrs. Grose appeared to study them! "But for what?"

"For the love of all the evil that, in those dreadful days, the pair put into them. And to ply them with that evil still, to keep up the work of demons, is what brings the others back."

"Laws!" said my friend under her breath. The exclamation was homely, but it revealed a real acceptance of my further proof of what, in the bad time—for there had been a worse even than this!—must have occurred. There could have been no such justification for me as the plain assent of her experience to whatever depth of depravity I found credible in our brace of scoundrels. It was in obvious submission of memory that she brought out after a moment: "They *were* rascals! But what can they now do?" she pursued.

"Do?" I echoed so loud that Miles and Flora, as they passed at their distance, paused an instant in their walk and looked at us. "Don't they do enough?" I demanded in a lower tone, while the children, having smiled and nodded and kissed hands to us, resumed their exhibition. We were held by it a minute; then I answered: "They can destroy them!" At this my companion did turn, but the inquiry she launched was a silent one, the effect of which was to make me more explicit. "They don't know, as yet, quite how—but they're trying hard. They're seen only across, as it were, and beyond—in strange places and on high places, the top of towers, the roof of houses, the outside of windows, the further edge of pools; but there's a deep design, on either side, to shorten the distance and overcome the obstacle; and the success of the tempters is only a question of time. They've only to keep to their suggestions of danger."

"For the children to come?"

"And perish in the attempt!" Mrs. Grose slowly got up, and I scrupulously added: "Unless, of course, we can prevent!"

Standing there before me while I kept my seat, she visibly turned things over. "Their uncle must do the preventing. He must take them away."

"And who's to make him?"

She had been scanning the distance, but she now dropped on me a foolish face. "You, Miss."

"By writing to him that his house is poisoned and his little nephew and niece mad?"

"But if they *are*, Miss?"

"And if I am myself, you mean? That's charming news to be sent him by a governess whose prime undertaking was to give him no worry."

Mrs. Grose considered, following the children again. "Yes, he do hate worry. That was the great reason——"

"Why those fiends took him in so long? No doubt, though his indifference must have been awful. As I'm not a fiend, at any rate, I shouldn't take him in."

My companion, after an instant and for all answer, sat

down again and grasped my arm. "Make him at any rate come to you."

I stared. "To *me?*" I had a sudden fear of what she might do. " 'Him'?"

"He ought to *be* here—he ought to help."

I quickly rose, and I think I must have shown her a queerer face than ever yet. "You see me asking him for a visit?" No, with her eyes on my face she evidently couldn't. Instead of it even—as a woman reads another—she could see what I myself saw: his derision, his amusement, his contempt for the break-down of my resignation at being left alone and for the fine machinery I had set in motion to attract his attention to my slighted charms. She didn't know—no one knew—how proud I had been to serve him and to stick to our terms; yet she none the less took the measure, I think, of the warning I now gave her. "If you should so lose your head as to appeal to him for me——"

She was really frightened. "Yes, Miss?"

"I would leave, on the spot, both him and you."

XIII

It was all very well to join them, but speaking to them proved quite as much as ever an effort beyond my strength —offered, in close quarters, difficulties as insurmountable as before. This situation continued a month, and with new aggravations and particular notes, the note above all, sharper and sharper, of the small ironic consciousness on the part of my pupils. It was not, I am as sure today as I was sure then, my mere infernal imagination: it was absolutely traceable that they were aware of my predicament and that this strange relation made, in a manner, for a long time, the air in which we moved. I don't mean that they had their tongues in their cheeks or did anything vulgar, for that was not one of their dangers: I do mean, on the other hand, that the element of the unnamed and untouched became, between us, greater than any other, and that so much avoidance could not have been so successfully effected without a great deal of tacit arrangement. It was as if, at moments, we were perpetually coming into sight of subjects before which we must stop short, turning suddenly out of alleys that we perceived to be blind, closing with a little bang that made us look at each other—for, like all bangs, it was something louder than we had intended—the doors we had indiscreetly opened. All roads lead to Rome, and there were times when it might have struck us that almost every branch of study or subject of conversation skirted forbidden ground. Forbidden ground was the question of the return of the dead in general and of whatever, in especial, might survive, in memory, of the friends little children had lost. There were days when I could have sworn that one of them had, with a small invisible nudge, said to the other: "She thinks she'll do it this time—but she *won't* !" To "do it" would have been to indulge for instance—and for once in a way—in some direct reference to the lady who had prepared them for my discipline. They had a delightful endless appetite for passages in my own history, to which I had again and again treated them; they were in possession of everything that had ever happened to me, had had, with every circumstance the story of my smallest adventures and of those of my brothers and sisters and of the cat and the dog at home, as well as many particulars of the eccentric nature of my father, of the furniture and arrangement of our house, and of the conversation of the old women of our village. There were things enough, taking one with another, to chatter about, if one went very fast and knew by instinct when to go round. They pulled with an art of their own the strings of my invention and my memory; and nothing else perhaps, when I thought of such occasions afterwards, gave me so the suspicion of being watched from under cover. It was in any case over *my* life, *my* past, and *my* friends alone that we could take anything like our ease—a state of affairs that led them sometimes without the least pertinence to break out into sociable reminders. I was invited—with no visible connection—to repeat afresh Goody Gosling's celebrated *mot* or to confirm the details already supplied as to the cleverness of the vicarage pony.

It was partly at such junctures as these and partly at quite different ones that, with the turn my matters had now taken, my predicament, as I have called it, grew most sensible. The fact that the days passed for me without another encounter ought, it would have appeared, to have done something toward soothing my nerves. Since the light brush, that second night on the upper landing, of the presence of a woman at the foot of the stair, I had seen nothing, whether in or out of the house, that one had better not have seen. There was many a corner round which I expected to come upon Quint, and many a situation that, in a merely sinister way, would have favoured the appearance of Miss Jessel. The summer had turned, the summer had gone; the autumn had dropped upon Bly and had blown out half our lights. The place, with its grey sky and withered garlands, its bared spaces and scattered dead leaves, was like a theatre after the performance—all strewn with crumpled playbills. There were exactly states of the air, conditions of sound and of stillness, unspeakable impressions of the *kind* of ministering moment, that brought back to me, long enough to catch it, the feeling of the medium in which, that June evening out-of-doors, I had had my first sight of Quint, and in which, too, at those other instants, I had, after seeing him through the window, looked for him in vain in the circle of shrubbery. I recognised the signs, the portents—I recognised the moment, the spot. But they remained unaccompanied and empty, and I continued unmolested; if unmolested one could call a young woman whose sensibility had, in the most extraordinary fashion, not declined but deepened. I had said in my talk with Mrs. Grose on that horrid scene of Flora's by the lake—and had perplexed her by so saying—that it would from that moment distress me much more to lose my power than to keep it. I had then expressed what was vividly in my mind: the truth that, whether the children really saw or not—since, that is, it was not yet definitely proved—I greatly preferred, as a safeguard, the fulness of my own exposure. I was ready to know the very worst that was to be known. What I had then had an ugly glimpse of was that my eyes might be sealed just while theirs were most opened. Well, my eyes *were* sealed, it appeared, at present—a consummation for which it seemed blasphemous not to thank God. There was, alas, a difficulty about that: I would have thanked him with all my soul had I not had in a proportionate measure this conviction of the secret of my pupils.

How can I retrace today the strange steps of my obsession? There were times of our being together when I would have been ready to swear that, literally, in my presence, but with my direct sense of it closed, they had visitors who were known and were welcome. Then it was that, had I not been deterred by the very chance that such an injury might prove greater than the injury to be averted, my exultation would have broken out. "They're here, they're here, you little wretches," I would have cried, "and you can't deny it now!" The little wretches denied it with all the added volume of their sociability and their tenderness, in just the crystal depths of which—like the flash of a fish in a stream—the mockery of their advantage peeped up. The shock, in truth, had sunk into me still deeper than I knew on the night when, looking out to see either Quint or Miss Jessel under the stars, I had beheld the boy over whose rest I watched and who had immediately brought in with him—had straightway, there, turned it on me—the lovely upward look with which, from the battlements above me, the hideous apparition of Quint had played. If it was a question of a scare, my discovery on this occasion had scared me more than any other, and it was in the condition of nerves produced by it that I made my actual inductions. They harassed me so that sometimes, at add moments, I shut myself up audibly to rehease—it was at once a fantastic relief and a renewed despair—the manner in which I might come to the point. I approached it from one side and the other while, in my room, I flung myself about, but I always broke down in the monstrous utterance of names. As they died away on my lips, I said to myself that I should indeed help them to represent something infamous if, by pronouncing them, I should violate as rare a little case of instinctive delicacy as any schoolroom, probably, had ever known. When I said to myself: "*They* have the manners to be silent, and you, trusted as you are, the baseness to speak!" I felt myself crimson and I covered my face with my hands. After these secret scenes I chattered more than ever, going on volubly enough 'til one of our prodigious, palpable hushes occurred—I can call

them nothing else—the strange, dizzy lift or swim (I try
for terms!) into a stillness, a pause of all life, that had
nothing to do with the more or less noise that at the moment we might be engaged in making and that I could
hear through any deepened exhilaration or quickened reci-
tation or louder strum of the piano. Then it was that the
others, the outsiders, were there. Though they were not
angels, they "passed," as the French say, causing me, while
they stayed, to tremble with the fear of their addressing to
their younger victims some yet more infernal message or
more vivid image than they had thought good enough for
myself.

What it was most impossible to get rid of was the cruel
idea that, whatever I had seen, Miles and Flora saw *more*
—things terrible and unguessable and that sprang from
dreadful passages of intercourse in the past. Such things
naturally left on the surface, for the time, a chill which
we vociferously denied that we felt; and we had, all three,
with repetition, got into such splendid training that we
went, each time, almost automatically, to mark the close
of the incident, through the very same movements. It was
striking of the children, at all events, to kiss me inveterately with a kind of wild irrelevance and never to fail—
one or the other—of the precious question that had helped
us through many a peril. "When do you think he *will*
come? Don't you think we *ought* to write?"—there was
nothing like that inquiry, we found by experience, for carrying off an awkwardness. "He" of course was their uncle
in Harley Street; and we lived in much profusion of theory
that he might at any moment arrive to mingle in our
circle. It was impossible to have given less encouragement
than he had done to such a doctrine, but if we had not had
the doctrine to fall back upon we should have deprived each
other of some of our finest exhibitions. He never wrote to
them—that may have been selfish, but it was a part of the
flattery of his trust of me; for the way in which a man
pays his highest tribute to a woman is apt to be but by

the more festal celebration of one of the sacred laws of
his comfort; and I held that I carried out the spirit of the
pledge given not to appeal to him when I let my charges
understand that their own letters were but charming literary exercises. They were too beautiful to be posted; I
kept them myself; I have them all to this hour. This was
a rule indeed which only added to the satiric effect of my
being plied with the supposition that he might at any
moment be among us. It was exactly as if my charges knew
how almost more awkward than anything else that might
be for me. There appears to me, moreover, as I look back,
no note in all this more extraordinary than the mere fact
that, in spite of my tension and of their triumph, I never
lost patience with them. Adorable they must in truth have
been, I now reflect, that I didn't in these days hate them!
Would exasperation, however, if relief had longer been
postponed, finally have betrayed me? It little matters, for
relief arrived. I call it relief, though it was only the relief
that a snap brings to a strain or the burst of a thunder-
storm to a day of suffocation. It was at least change, and
it came with a rush.

XIV

WALKING to church a certain Sunday morning, I had little Miles at my side and his sister, in advance of us and at Mrs. Grose's, well in sight. It was a crisp, clear day, the first of its order for some time; the night had brought a touch of frost, and the autumn air, bright and sharp, made the church-bells almost gay. It was an odd accident of thought that I should have happened at such a moment to be particularly and very gratefully struck with the obedience of my little charges. Why did they never resent my inexhorable, my perpetual society? Something or other had brought nearer home to me that I had all but pinned the boy to my shawl and that, in the way our companions were marshalled before me, I might have appeared to provide against some danger of rebellion. I was like a gaoler with an eye to possible surprises and escapes. But all this belonged—I mean their magnificent little surrender—just to the special array of the facts that were most abysmal. Turned out for Sunday by his uncle's tailor, who had had a free hand and a notion of pretty waistcoats and of his grand little air, Miles's whole title to independence, the rights of his sex and situation, were so stamped upon him that if he had suddenly struck for freedom I should have had nothing to say. I was by the strangest of chances wondering how I should meet him when the revolution unmistakeably occurred. I call it a revolution because I now see how, with the word he spoke, the curtain rose on the last act of my dreadful drama and the catastrophe was precipitated. "Look here, my dear, you know," he charmingly said, "when in the world, please, am I going back to school?"

Transcribed here the speech sounds harmless enough.

particularly as uttered in the sweet, high, casual pipe with which, at all interlocutors, but above all at his eternal governess, he threw off intonations as if he were tossing roses. There was something in them that always made one "catch," and I caught, at any rate, now so effectually that I stopped as short as if one of the trees of the park had fallen across the road. There was something new, on the spot, between us, and he was perfectly aware that I recognised it, though, to enable me to do so, he had no need to look a whit less candid and charming than usual. I could feel in him how he already, from my at first finding nothing to reply, perceived the advantage he had gained. I was so slow to find anything that he had plenty of time, after a minute, to continue with his suggestive but inconclusive smile: "You know, my dear, that for a fellow to be with a lady *always*——!" His "my dear" was constantly on his lips for me, and nothing could have expressed more the exact shade of the sentiment with which I desired to inspire my pupils than its fond familiarity. It was so respectfully easy.

But, oh, how I felt that at present I must pick my own phrases! I remember that, to gain time, I tried to laugh, and I seemed to see in the beautiful face with which he watched me how ugly and queer I looked. "And always with the same lady?" I returned.

He neither blenched nor winked. The whole thing was virtually out between us. "Ah, of course, she's a jolly, 'perfect' lady; but, after all, I'm a fellow, don't you see? that's—well, getting on."

I lingered there with him an instant ever so kindly. "Yes, you're getting on." Oh, but I felt helpless!

I have kept to this day the heartbreaking little idea of how he seemed to know that and to play with it. "And you can't say I've not been awfully good, can you?"

I laid my hand on his shoulder, for, though I felt how much better it would have been to walk on, I was not yet quite able. "No, I can't say that, Miles."

"Except just that one night, you know——!"

"That one night?" I couldn't look as straight as he.

"Why, when I went down—went out of the house."

"Oh, yes. But I forget what you did it for."

"You forget?"—he spoke with the sweet extravagance of childish reproach. "Why, it was to show you I could!"

"Oh, yes, you could."

"And I can again."

I felt that I might, perhaps, after all succeed in keeping my wits about me. "Certainly. But you won't."

"No, not *that* again. It was nothing."

"It was nothing," I said. "But we must go on."

He resumed our walk with me, passing his hand into my arm. "Then when *am* I going back?"

I wore, in turning it over, my most responsible air. "Were you very happy at school?"

He just considered. "Oh, I'm happy enough anywhere!"

"Well, then," I quavered, "if you're just as happy here ——!"

"Ah, but that isn't everything! Of course *you* know a lot——"

"But you hint that you know almost as much?" I risked as he paused.

"Not half I want to!" Miles honestly professed. "But it isn't so much that."

"What is it, then?"

"Well—I want to see more life."

"I see; I see." We had arrived within sight of the church and of various persons, including several of the household of Bly, on their way to it and clustered about the door to see us go in. I quickened our step; I wanted to get there before the question between us opened up much further; I reflected hungrily that, for more than an hour, he would have to be silent; and I thought with envy of the comparative dusk of the pew and of the almost spiritual help of the hassock on which I might bend my knees. I seemed literally to be running a race with some

confusion to which he was about to reduce me, but I felt
that he had got in first when, before we had even entered
the churchyard, he threw out—

"I want my own sort!"

It literally made me bound forward. "There are not
many of your own sort, Miles!" I laughed. "Unless perhaps dear little Flora!"

"You really compare me to a baby girl?"

This found me singularly weak. "Don't you, then, *love*
our sweet Flora?"

"If I didn't—and you too; if I didn't——!" he repeated
as if retreating for a jump, yet leaving his thought so un-
finished that, after we had come into the gate, another
stop, which he imposed on me by the pressure of his arm,
had become inevitable. Mrs. Grose and Flora had passed
into the church, the other worshippers had followed, and
we were, for the minute, alone among the old, thick
graves. We had paused, on the path from the gate, by a
low, oblong, table-like tomb.

"Yes, if you didn't——?"

He looked, while I waited, about at the graves. "Well,
you know what!" But he didn't move, and he presently
produced something that made me drop straight down on
the stone slab, as if suddenly to rest. "Does my uncle
think what *you* think?"

I markedly rested. "How do you know what I think?"

"Ah, well, of course I don't; for it strikes me you never
tell me. But I mean does *he* know?"

"Know what, Miles?"

"Why, the way I'm going on."

I perceived quickly enough that I could make, to this
inquiry, no answer that would not involve something of a
sacrifice of my employer. Yet it appeared to me that we
were all, at Bly, sufficiently sacrificed to make that venial.
"I don't think your uncle much cares."

Miles, on this, stood looking at me. "Then don't you
think he can be made to?"

"In what way?"

"Why, by his coming down.'

"But who'll get him to come down?"

"*I* will!" the boy said with extraordinary brightness and emphasis. He gave me another look charged with that expression and then marched off alone into church.

XV

THE business was practically settled from the moment
I never followed him. It was a pitiful surrender to agitation, but my being aware of this had somehow no power
to restore me. I only sat there on my tomb and read into
what my little friend had said to me the fulness of its
meaning; by the time I had grasped the whole of which I
had also embraced, for absence, the pretext that I was
ashamed to offer my pupils and the rest of the congrega-
tion such an example of delay. What I said to myself above
all was that Miles had got something out of me and that
the proof of it, for him, would be just this awkward collapse. He had got out of me that there was something I
was much afraid of and that he should probably be able
to make use of my fear to gain, for his own purpose, more
freedom. My fear was of having to deal with the intolerable question of the grounds of his dismissal from school,
for that was really but the question of the horrors gathered
behind. That his uncle should arrive to treat with me of
these things was a solution that, strictly speaking, I ought
now to have desired to bring on; but I could so little face
the ugliness and the pain of it that I simply procrasti-
nated and lived from hand to mouth. The boy, to my deep
discomposure, was immensely in the right, was in a position to say to me: "Either you clear up with my guardian
the mystery of this interruption of my studies, or you cease
to expect me to lead with you a life that's so unnatural
for a boy." What was so unnatural for the particular boy
I was concerned with was this sudden revelation of a
consciousness and a plan.

That was what really overcame me, what prevented my
going in. I walked round the church, hesitating, hover-

ing; I reflected that I had already, with him, hurt myself beyond repair. Therefore I could patch up nothing, and it was too extreme an effort to squeeze beside him into the pew: he would be so much more sure than ever to pass his arm into mine and make me sit there for an hour in close, silent contact with his commentary on our talk. For the first minute since his arrival I wanted to get away from him. As I paused beneath the high east window and listened to the sounds of worship, I was taken with an impulse that might master me, I felt, completely should I give it the least encouragement. I might easily put an end to my predicament by getting away altogether. Here was my chance; there was no one to stop me; I could give the whole thing up—turn my back and retreat. It was only a question of hurrying again, for a few preparations, to the house which the attendance at church of so many of the servants would practically have left unoccupied. No, one, in short, could blame me if I should just drive desperately off. What was it to get away if I got away only till dinner? That would be in a couple of hours, at the end of which—I had the acute prevision—my little pupils would play at innocent wonder about my non-appearance in their train.

"What *did* you do, you naughty, bad thing? Why in the world, to worry us so—and take our thoughts off too, don't you know?—did you desert us at the very door?" I couldn't meet such questions nor, as they asked them, their false little lovely eyes; yet it was all so exactly what I should have to meet that, as the prospect grew sharp to me, I at last let myself go.

I got, so far as the immediate moment was concerned, away; I came straight out of the churchyard and, thinking hard, retraced my steps through the park. It seemed to me that by the time I reached the house I had made up my mind I would fly. The Sunday stillness both of the approaches and of the interior, in which I met no one, fairly excited me with a sense of opportunity. Were I to

get off quickly, this way, I should get off without a scene,
without a word. My quickness would have to be remarkable, however, and the question of a conveyance was the
great one to settle. Tormented, in the hall, with difficulties and obstacles, I remember sinking down at the foot
of the staircase—suddenly collapsing there on the lowest
step and then, with a revulsion, recalling that it was exactly where more than a month before, in the darkness of
night and just so bowed with evil things, I had seen the
spectre of the most horrible of women. At this I was able
to straighten myself; I went the rest of the way up; I
made, in my bewilderment, for the schoolroom, where
there were objects belonging to me that I should have to
take. But I opened the door to find again, in a flash, my
eyes unsealed. In the presence of what I saw I reeled
straight back upon my resistance.

Seated at my own table in clear noonday light I saw a
person whom, without my previous experience, I should
have taken at the first blush for some housemaid who
might have stayed at home to look after the place and
who, availing herself of rare relief from observation and
of the schoolroom table and my pens, ink, and paper, had
applied herself to the considerable effort of a letter to
her sweetheart. There was an effort in the way that, while
her arms rested on the table, her hands with evident weari-
ness supported her head; but at the moment I took this
in I had already become aware that, in spite of my entrance, her attitude strangely persisted. Then it was—
with the very act of its announcing itself—that her identity flared up in a change of posture. She rose, not as if
she had heard me, but with an indescribable grand melancholy of indifference and detachment, and, within a
dozen feet of me, stood there as my vile predecessor. Dis-
honoured and tragic, she was all before me; but even as I
fixed and, for memory, secured it, the awful image passed
away. Dark as midnight in her black dress, her haggard
beauty and her unutterable woe, she had looked at me

long enough to appear to say that her right to sit at my table was as good as mine to sit at hers. While these instants lasted indeed I had the extraordinary chill of a feeling that it was I who was the intruder. It was as a wild protest against it that, actually addressing her—"You terrible, miserable woman!"—I heard myself break into a sound that, by the open door, rang through the long passage and the empty house. She looked at me as if she heard me, but I had recovered myself and cleared the air. There was nothing in the room the next minute but the sunshine and a sense that I must stay.

XVI

I HAD so perfectly expected that the return of my pupils would be marked by a demonstration that I was freshly upset at having to take into account that they were dumb about my absence. Instead of gaily denouncing and caressing me, they made no allusion to my having failed them, and I was left, for the time, on perceiving that she too said nothing, to study Mrs. Grose's odd face. I did this to such purpose that I made sure they had in some way bribed her to silence; a silence that, however, I would engage to break down on the first private opportunity. This opportunity came before tea: I secured five minutes with her in the housekeeper's room, where, in the twilight, amid a smell of lately-baked bread, but with the place all swept and garnished, I found her sitting in pained placidity before the fire. So I see her still, so I see her best: facing the flame from her straight chair in the dusky, shining room, a large clean image of the "put away"— of drawers closed and locked and rest without a remedy.

"Oh, yes, they asked me to say nothing; and to please them—so long as they were there—of course I promised. But what had happened to you?"

"I only went with you for the walk," I said. "I had then to come back to meet a friend."

She showed her surprise. "A friend—*you?*"

"Oh, yes, I have a couple!" I laughed. "But did the children give you a reason?"

"For not alluding to your leaving us? Yes; they said you would like it better. Do you like it better?"

My face had made her rueful. "No, I like it worse!" But after an instant I added: "Did they say why I should like it better?"

"No; Master Miles only said, 'We must do nothing but what she likes'!"

"I wish indeed he would! And what did Flora say?"

"Miss Flora was too sweet. She said, 'Oh, of course, of course!'—and I said the same."

I thought a moment. "You were too sweet too—I can hear you all. But none the less, between Miles and me, it's now all out."

"All out?" My companion stared. "But what, Miss?"

"Everything. It doesn't matter. I've made up my mind. I came home, my dear," I went on, "for a talk with Miss Jessel."

I had by this time formed the habit of having Mrs. Grose literally well in hand in advance of my sounding that note; so that even now, as she bravely blinked under the signal of my word, I could keep her comparatively firm. "A talk! Do you mean she spoke?"

"It came to that. I found her, on my return, in the schoolroom."

"And what did she say?" I can hear the good woman still, and the candour of her stupefaction.

"That she suffers the torments——!"

It was this, of a truth, that made her, as she filled out my picture gape. "Do you mean," she faltered, "—of the lost?"

"Of the lost. Of the damned. And that's why, to share them——" I faltered myself with the horror of it.

But my companion, with less imagination, kept me up. "To share them——?"

"She wants Flora." Mrs. Grose might, as I gave it to her, fairly have fallen away from me had I not been prepared. I still held her there, to show I was. "As I've told you, however, it doesn't matter."

"Because you've made up your mind? But to what?"

"To everything."

"And what do you call 'everything'?"

"Why, sending for their uncle."

"Oh, Miss, in pity do," my friend broke out.

"Ah, but I will, I *will!* I see it's the only way. What's 'out,' as I told you, with Miles is that if he thinks I'm afraid to—and has ideas of what he gains by that—he shall see he's mistaken. Yes, yes; his uncle shall have it here from me on the spot (and before the boy himself if necessary) that if I'm to be reproached with having done nothing again about more school——"

"Yes, Miss——" my companion pressed me.

"Well, there's that awful reason."

There were now clearly so many of these for my poor colleague that she was excusable for being vague. "But —a—which?"

"Why, the letter from his old place."

"You'll show it to the master?"

"I ought to have done so on the instant."

"Oh, no!" said Mrs. Grose with decision.

"I'll put it before him," I went on inexorably, "that I can't undertake to work the question on behalf of a child who has been expelled——"

"For we've never in the least known what!" Mrs. Grose declared.

"For wickedness. For what else—when he's so clever and beautiful and perfect? Is he stupid? Is he untidy? Is he infirm? Is he ill-natured? He's exquisite—so it can be only *that;* and that would open up the whole thing. After all," I said, "it's their uncle's fault. If he left here such people——!"

"He didn't really in the least know them. The fault's mine." She had turned quite pale.

"Well, you shan't suffer," I answered.

"The children shan't!" she emphatically returned.

I was silent awhile; we looked at each other. "Then what am I to tell him?"

"You needn't tell him anything. *I'll* tell him.

I measured this. "Do you mean you'll write——?" Remembering she couldn't, I caught myself up. "How do you communicate?"

"I tell the bailiff. *He* writes."

"And should you like him to write our story?"

My question had a sarcastic force that I had not fully intended, and it made her, after a moment, inconsequently break down. The tears were again in her eyes. "Ah, Miss, *you* write!"

"Well—tonight," I at last answered; and on this we separated.

XVII

I WENT so far, in the evening, as to make a beginning. The weather had changed back, a great wind was abroad, and beneath the lamp, in my room, with Flora at peace beside me, I sat for a long time before a blank sheet of paper and listened to the lash of the rain and the batter of the gusts. Finally I went out, taking a candle; I crossed the passage and listened a minute at Miles's door. What, under my endless obsession, I had been impelled to listen for was some betrayal of his not being at rest, and I presently caught one, but not in the form I had expected. His voice tinkled out. "I say, you there—come in." It was a gaiety in the gloom!

I went in with my light and found him, in bed, very wide awake, but very much at his ease. "Well, what are *you* up to?" he asked with a grace of sociability in which it occurred to me that Mrs. Grose, had she been present, might have looked in vain for proof that anything was "out."

I stood over him with my candle. "How did you know I was there?"

"Why, of course I heard you. Did you fancy you made no noise? You're like a troop of cavalry!" he beautifully laughed.

"Then you weren't asleep?"

"Not much! I lie awake and think."

I had put my candle, designedly, a short way off, and then, as he held out his friendly old hand to me, had sat down on the edge of his bed. "What is it," I asked, "that you think of?"

"What in the world, my dear, but *you?*"

"Ah, the pride I take in your appreciation doesn't insist on that! I had so far rather you slept."

"Well, I think also, you know, of this queer business of ours."

I marked the coolness of his firm little hand. "Of what queer business, Miles?"

"Why, the way you bring me up. And all the rest!"

I fairly held my breath a minute, and even from my glimmering taper there was light enough to show how he smiled up at me from his pillow. "What do you mean by all the rest?"

"Oh, you know, you know!"

I could say nothing for a minute, though I felt, as I held his hand and our eyes continued to meet, that my silence had all the air of admitting his charge and that nothing in the whole world of reality was perhaps at that moment so fabulous as our actual relation. "Certainly you shall go back to school," I said, "if it be that that troubles you. But not to the old place—we must find another, a better. How could I know it did trouble you, this question, when you never told me so, never spoke of it at all?" His clear, listening face, framed in its smooth whiteness, made him for the minute as appealing as some wistful patient in a children's hospital; and I would have given, as the resemblance came to me, all I possessed on earth really to be the nurse or the sister of charity who might have helped to cure him. Well, even as it was, I perhaps might help! "Do you know you've never said a word to me about your school—I mean the old one; never mentioned it in any way?"

He seemed to wonder; he smiled with the same loveliness. But he clearly gained time; he waited, he called for guidance. "Haven't I?" It wasn't for *me* to help him—it was for the thing I had met!

Something in his tone and the expression of his face, as I got this from him, set my heart aching with such a pang as it had never yet known; so unutterably touching was it to see his little brain puzzled and his little resources taxed to play, under the spell laid on him, a part of innocence and consistency. "No, never—from the hour you came back. You've never mentioned to me one of your masters, one of your comrades, nor the least little thing that ever happened to you at school. Never, little Miles— no, never—have you given me an inkling of anything that *may* have happened there. Therefore you can fancy how much I'm in the dark. Until you came out, that way, this morning, you had, since the first hour I saw you, scarce even made a reference to anything in your previous life. You seemed so perfectly to accept the present." It was extraordinary how my absolute conviction of his secret precocity (or whatever I might call the poison of an influence that I dared but half to phrase) made him, in spite of the faint breath of his inward trouble, appear as accessible as an older person—imposed him almost as an intellectual equal. "I thought you wanted to go on as you are."

It struck me that at this he just faintly coloured. He gave, at any rate, like a convalescent slightly fatigued, a languid shake of his head. "I don't—I don't. I want to get away."

"You're tired of Bly?"

"Oh, no, I like Bly."

"Well, then——?"

"Oh, *you* know what a boy wants!"

I felt that I didn't know so well as Miles, and I took temporary refuge. "You want to go to your uncle?"

Again, at this, with his sweet ironic face, he made a movement on the pillow. "Ah, you can't get off with that!"

I was silent a little, and it was I, now, I think, who changed colour. "My dear, I don't want to get off!"

"You can't, even if you do. You can't, you can't!"—he lay beautifully staring. "My uncle must come down, and you must completely settle things."

"If we do," I returned with some spirit, "you may be sure it will be to take you quite away."

"Well, don't you understand that that's exactly what I'm working for? You'll have to tell him—about the way you've let it all drop: you'll have to tell him a tremendous lot!"

The exultation with which he uttered this helped me somehow, for the instant, to meet him rather more. "And how much will *you*, Miles, have to tell him? There are things he'll ask you!"

He turned it over. "Very likely. But what things?"

"The things you've never told me. To make up his mind what to do with you. He can't send you back——"

"Oh, I don't want to go back!" he broke in. "I want a new field."

He said it with admirable serenity, with positive unimpeachable gaiety; and doubtless it was that very note that most evoked for me the poignancy, the unnatural childish tragedy, of his probable reappearance at the end of three months with all this bravado and still more dishonour. It overwhelmed me now that I should never be able to bear that, and it made me let myself go. I threw myself upon him and in the tenderness of my pity I embraced him. "Dear little Miles, dear little Miles——!"

My face was close to his, and he let me kiss him, simply taking it with indulgent good-humour. "Well, old lady?"

"Is there nothing—nothing at all that you want to tell me?"

He turned off a little, facing round toward the wall and holding up his hand to look at as one had seen sick children look. "I've told you—I told you this morning."

Oh, I was sorry for him! "That you just want me not to worry you?"

He looked round at me now, as if in recognition of my understanding him; then ever so gently, "To let me alone," he replied.

There was even a singular little dignity in it, something

that made me release him, yet, when I had slowly risen, linger beside him. God knows I never wished to harass him, but I felt that merely, at this, to turn my back on him was to abandon or, to put it more truly, to lose him. "I've just begun a letter to your uncle," I said.

"Well, then, finish it!"

I waited a minute. "What happened before?"

He gazed up at me again. "Before what?"

"Before you came back. And before you went away."

For some time he was silent, but he continued to meet my eyes. "What happened?"

It made me, the sound of the words, in which it seemed to me that I caught for the very first time a small faint quaver of consenting consciousness—it made me drop on my knees beside the bed and seize once more the chance of possessing him. "Dear little Miles, dear little Miles, if you *knew* how I want to help you! It's only that, it's nothing but that, and I'd rather die than give you a pain or do you a wrong—I'd rather die than hurt a hair of you. Dear little Miles"—oh, I brought it out now even if I *should* go too far—"I just want you to help me to save you!" But I knew in a moment after this that I had gone too far. The answer to my appeal was instantaneous, but it came in the form of an extraordinary blast and chill, a gust of frozen air and a shake of the room as great as if, in the wild wind, the casement had crashed in. The boy gave a loud, high shriek, which, lost in the rest of the shock of sound, might have seemed, indistinctly, though I was so close to him, a note either of jubilation or of terror. I jumped to my feet again and was conscious of darkness. So for a moment we remained, while I stared about me and saw that the drawn curtains were unstirred and the window tight. "Why, the candle's out!" I then cried.

"It was I who blew it, dear!" said Miles.

XVIII

THE next day, after lessons, Mrs. Grose found a moment to say to me quietly: "Have you written, Miss?"

"Yes—I've written." But I didn't add—for the hour—that my letter, sealed and directed, was still in my pocket. There would be time enough to send it before the messenger should go to the village. Meanwhile there had been, on the part of my pupils, no more brilliant, more exemplary morning. It was exactly as if they had both had at heart to gloss over any recent little friction. They performed the dizziest feats of arithmetic, soaring quite out of *my* feeble range, and perpetrated, in higher spirits than ever, geographical and historical jokes. It was conspicuous of course in Miles in particular that he appeared to wish to show how easily he could let me down. This child, to my memory, really lives in a setting of beauty and misery that no words can translate; there was a distinction all his own in every impulse he revealed; never was a small natural creature, to the uninitiated eye all frankness and freedom, a more ingenious, a more extraordinary little gentleman. I had perpetually to guard against the wonder of contemplation into which my initiated view betrayed me; to check the irrelevant gaze and discouraged sigh in which I constantly both attacked and renounced the enigma of what such a little gentleman could have done that deserved a penalty. Say that, by the dark prodigy I knew, the imagination of all evil *had* been opened up to him: all the justice within me ached for the proof that it could ever have flowered into an act.

He had never, at any rate, been such a little gentleman as when, after our early dinner on this dreadful day, he came round to me and asked if I shouldn't like him, for half an hour, to play to me. David playing to Saul could never have shown a finer sense of the occasion. It was literally a charming exhibition of tact, of magnanimity, and quite tantamount to his saying outright: "The true knights we love to read about never push an advantage too far. I know what you mean now: you mean that— to be let alone yourself and not followed up—you'll cease to worry and spy upon me, won't keep me so close to you, will let me go and come. Well, I 'come,' you see—but I don't go! There'll be plenty of time for that. I do really delight in your society, and I only want to show you that I contended for a principle." It may be imagined whether I resisted this appeal or failed to accompany him again, hand in hand, to the schoolroom. He sat down at the old piano and played as he had never played, and if there are those who think he had better have been kicking a football I can only say that I wholly agree with them. For at the end of a time that under his influence I had quite ceased to measure I started up with a strange sense of having literally slept at my post. It was after luncheon, and by the schoolroom fire, and yet I hadn't really, in the least, slept: I had only done something much worse—I had forgotten. Where, all this time, was Flora? When I put the question to Miles he played on a minute before answering, and then could only say: "Why, my dear, how do I know?"—breaking moreover into a happy laugh which, immediately after, as if it were a vocal accompaniment, he prolonged into incoherent, extravagant song.

I went straight to my room, but his sister was not there; then, before going downstairs, I looked into several others. As she was nowhere about she would surely be with Mrs. Grose, whom, in the comfort of that theory, I accordingly proceeded in quest of. I found her where I had found her the evening before, but she met my quick challenge with blank, scared ignorance. She had only supposed that, after the repast, I had carried off both the children; as to which she was quite in her right, for it was the very first time

I had allowed the little girl out of my sight without some
special provision. Of course now indeed she might be with
the maids, so that the immediate thing was to look for
her without an air of alarm. This we promptly arranged
between us; but when, ten minutes later and in pursuance
of our arrangement, we met in the hall, it was only to
report on either side that after guarded inquiries we had
altogether failed to trace her. For a minute there, apart
from observation, we exchanged mute alarms, and I could
feel with what high interest my friend returned me all
those I had from the first given her.

"She'll be above," she presently said—"in one of the
rooms you haven't searched."

"No; she's at a distance." I had made up my mind.
"She has gone out."

Mrs. Grose stared. "Without a hat?"

I naturally also looked volumes. "Isn't that woman
always without one?"

"She's with *her?*"

"She's with *her!*" I declared. "We must find them."

My hand was on my friend's arm, but she failed for the
moment, confronted with such an account of the matter,
to respond to my pressure. She communed, on the contrary, on the spot, with her uneasiness. "And where's
Master Miles?"

"Oh, *he's* with Quint. They're in the schoolroom."

"Lord, Miss!" My view, I was myself aware—and
therefore I suppose my tone—had never yet reached so
calm an assurance.

"The trick's played," I went on; "they've successfully
worked their plan. He found the most divine little way to
keep me quiet while she went off."

"'Divine'?" Mrs. Grose bewilderedly echoed.

"Infernal, then!" I almost cheerfully rejoined. "He has
provided for himself as well. But come!"

She had helplessly gloomed at the upper regions. "You
leave him——?"

"So long with Quint? Yes—I don't mind that now."

She always ended, at these moments, by getting posses-sion of my hand, and in this manner she could at present still stay me. But after gasping an instant at my sudden resignation, "Because of your letter?" she eagerly brought out.

I quickly, by way of answer, felt for my letter, drew it forth, held it up, and then, freeing myself, went and laid it on the great hall-table. "Luke will take it," I said as I came back. I reached the house-door and opened it; I was already on the steps.

My companion still demurred: the storm of the night and the early morning had dropped, but the afternoon was damp and grey. I came down to the drive while she stood in the doorway. "You go with nothing on?"

"What do I care when the child has nothing? I can't wait to dress," I cried, "and if you must do so, I leave you. Try meanwhile, yourself, upstairs."

"With *them?*" Oh, on this, the poor woman promptly joined me!

XIX

WE went straight to the lake, as it was called at Bly, and I dare say rightly called, though I reflect that it may in fact have been a sheet of water less remarkable than it appeared to my untravelled eyes. My acquaintance with sheets of water was small, and the pool of Bly, at all events on the few occasions of my consenting, under the protection of my pupils, to affront its surface in the old flat-bottomed boat moored there for our use, had impressed me both with its extent and its agitation. The usual place of embarkation was half a mile from the house, but I had an intimate conviction that, wherever Flora might be, she was not near home. She had not given me the slip for any small adventure, and, since the day of the very great one that I had shared with her by the pond, I had been aware, in our walks, of the quarter to which she most inclined. This was why I had now given to Mrs. Grose's steps so marked a direction—a direction that made her, when she perceived it, oppose a resistance that showed me she was freshly mystified. "You're going to the water, Miss?—you think she's *in*——?"

"She may be, though the depth is, I believe, nowhere very great. But what I judge most likely is that she's on the spot from which, the other day, we saw together what I told you."

"When she pretended not to see——?"

"With that astounding self-possession! I've always been sure she wanted to go back alone. And now her brother has managed it for her."

Mrs. Grose still stood where she had stopped. "You suppose they really *talk* of them?"

I could meet this with a confidence! "They say things that, if we heard them, would simply appall us."

"And if she *is* there——?"

"Yes?"

"Then Miss Jessel is?"

"Beyond a doubt. You shall see."

"Oh, thank you!" my friend cried, planted so firm that, taking it in, I went straight on without her. By the time I reached the pool, however, she was close behind me, and I knew that, whatever, to her apprehension, might befall me, the exposure of my society struck her as her least danger. She exhaled a moan of relief as we at last came in sight of the greater part of the water without a sight of the child. There was no trace of Flora on that nearer side of the bank where my observation of her had been most startling, and none on the opposite edge, where, save for a margin of some twenty yards, a thick copse came down to the water. The pond, oblong in shape, had a width so scant compared to its length that, with its ends out of view, it might have been taken for a scant river. We looked at the empty expanse, and then I felt the suggestion of my friend's eyes. I knew what she meant and I replied with a negative headshake.

"No, no; wait! She has taken the boat."

My companion stared at the vacant mooring-place and then again across the lake. "Then where is it?"

"Our not seeing it is the strongest of proofs. She has used it to go over, and then has managed to hide it."

"All alone—that child?"

"She's not alone, and at such times she's not a child: she's an old, old woman." I scanned all the visible shore while Mrs. Grose took again, into the queer element I offered her, one of her plunges of submission; then I pointed out that the boat might perfectly be in a small refuge formed by one of the recesses of the pool, an indentation masked, for the hither side, by a projection of the bank and by a clump of trees growing close to the water.

"But if the boat's there, where on earth's *she?*" my colleague anxiously asked.

"That's exactly what we must learn." And I started to walk further.

"By going all the way round?"

"Certainly, far as it is. It will take us but ten minutes, but it's far enough to have made the child prefer not to walk. She went straight over."

"Laws!" cried my friend again; the chain of my logic was ever too much for her. It dragged her at my heels even now, and when we had got half-way round—a devious, tiresome process, on ground much broken and by a path choked with overgrowth—I paused to give her breath. I sustained her with a grateful arm, assuring her that she might hugely help me; and this started us afresh, so that in the course of but few minutes more we reached a point from which we found the boat to be where I had supposed it. It had been intentionally left as much as possible out of sight and was tied to one of the stakes of a fence that came, just there, down to the brink and that had been an assistance to disembarking. I recognised, as I looked at the pair of short, thick oars, quite safely drawn up, the prodigious character of the feat for a little girl; but I had lived, by this time, too long among wonders and had panted to too many livelier measures. There was a gate in the fence, through which we passed, and that brought us, after a trifling interval, more into the open. Then, "There she is!" we both exclaimed at once.

Flora, a short way off, stood before us on the grass and smiled as if her performance was now complete. The next thing she did, however, was to stoop straight down and pluck—quite as if it were all she was there for—a big, ugly spray of withered fern. I instantly became sure she had just come out of the copse. She waited for us, not herself taking a step, and I was conscious of the rare solemnity with which we presently approached her. She smiled and smiled, and we met; but it was all done in a

silence by this time flagrantly ominous. Mrs. Grose was
the first to break the spell: she threw herself on her knees
and, drawing the child to her breast, clasped in a long
embrace the little tender, yielding body. While this dumb
convulsion lasted I could only watch it—which I did the
more intently when I saw Flora's face peep at me over our
companion's shoulder. It was serious now—the flicker had
left it; but it strengthened the pang with which I at that
moment envied Mrs. Grose the simplicity of *her* relation.
Still, all this while, nothing more passed between us save
that Flora had let her foolish fern again drop to the
ground. What she and I had virtually said to each other
was that pretexts were useless now. When Mrs. Grose
finally got up she kept the child's hand, so that the two
were still before me; and the singular reticence of our
communion was even more marked in the frank look she
launched me. "I'll be hanged," it said, "if *I'll* speak!"

It was Flora who, gazing all over me in candid wonder,
was the first. She was struck with our bareheaded aspect.
"Why, where are your things?"

"Where yours are, my dear!" I promptly returned.

She had already got back her gaiety, and appeared to
take this as an answer quite sufficient. "And where's
Miles?" she went on.

There was something in the small valour of it that
quite finished me: these three words from her were, in a
flash like the glitter of a drawn blade, the jostle of the
cup that my hand, for weeks and weeks, had held high
and full to the brim and that now, even before speaking,
I felt overflow in a deluge. "I'll tell you if you'll tell
me——" I heard myself say, then heard the tremor in
which it broke.

"Well, what?"

Mrs. Grose's suspense blazed at me, but it was too late
now, and I brought the thing out handsomely. "Where,
my pet, is Miss Jessel?"

XX

Just as in the churchyard with Miles, the whole thing was upon us. Much as I had made of the fact that this name had never once, between us, been sounded, the quick, smitten glare with which the child's face now received it fairly likened my breach of the silence to the smash of a pane of glass. It added to the interposing cry, as if to stay the blow, that Mrs. Grose, at the same instant, uttered over my violence—the shriek of a creature scared, or rather wounded, which, in turn, within a few seconds, was completed by a gasp of my own. I seized my colleague's arm. "She's there, she's there!"

Miss Jessel stood before us on the opposite bank exactly as she had stood the other time, and I remember, strangely, as the first feeling now produced in me, my thrill of joy at having brought on a proof. She was there, and I was justified; she was there, and I was neither cruel nor mad. She was there for poor scared Mrs. Grose, but she was there most for Flora; and no moment of my monstrous time was perhaps so extraordinary as that in which I consciously threw out to her—with the sense that, pale and ravenous demon as she was, she would catch and understand it—an inarticulate message of gratitude. She rose erect on the spot my friend and I had lately quitted, and there was not, in all the long reach of her desire, an inch of her evil that fell short. This first vividness of vision and emotion were things of a few seconds, during which Mrs. Grose's dazed blink across to where I pointed struck me as a sovereign sign that she too at last saw, just as it carried my own eyes precipitately to the child. The revelation then of the manner in which Flora was affected startled me, in truth, far more than it would have done to find her also merely agitated, for direct dismay was of course not what I had expected. Prepared and on her guard as our pursuit had actually made her, she would repress every betrayal; and I was therefore shaken, on the spot, by my first glimpse of the particular one for which I had not allowed. To see her, without a convulsion of her small pink face, not even feign to glance in the direction of the prodigy I announced, but only, instead of that, turn at *me* an expression of hard, still gravity, an expression absolutely new and unprecedented and that appeared to read and accuse and judge me— this was a stroke that somehow converted the little girl herself into the very presence that could make me quail. I quailed even though my certitude that she thoroughly saw was never greater than at that instant, and in the immediate need to defend myself I called it passionately to witness. "She's there, you little unhappy thing—there, there, *there*, and you see her as well as you see me!" I had said shortly before to Mrs. Grose that she was not at these times a child, but an old, old woman, and that description of her could not have been more strikingly confirmed than in the way in which, for all answer to this, she simply showed me, without a concession, an admission, of her eyes, a countenance of deeper and deeper, of indeed suddenly quite fixed, reprobation. I was by this time—if I can put the whole thing at all together—more appalled at what I may properly call her manner than at anything else, though it was simultaneously with this that I became aware of having Mrs. Grose also, and very formidably, to reckon with. My elder companion, the next moment, at any rate, blotted out everything but her own flushed face and her loud, shocked protest, a burst of high disapproval. "What a dreadful turn, to be sure, Miss! Where on earth do you see anything?"

I could only grasp her more quickly yet, for even while she spoke the hideous plain presence stood undimmed and undaunted. It had already lasted a minute, and lasted while I continued, seizing my colleague, quite thrusting her at it and presenting her to it, to insist with my pointing hand. "You don't see her exactly as *we* see? —you mean to say you don't now—*now?* She's as big as a blazing fire! Only look, dearest woman, *look*——!" She looked, even as I did, and gave me, with her deep groan of negation, repulsion, compassion—the mixture with her pity of her relief at her exemption—a sense, touching to me even then, that she would have backed me up if she could. I might well have needed that, for with this hard blow of the proof that her eyes were hopelessly sealed I felt my own situation horribly crumble, I felt—I saw— my livid predecessor press, from her position, on my defeat, and I was conscious, more than all, of what I should have from this instant to deal with in the astounding little attitude of Flora. Into this attitude Mrs. Grose immediately and violently entered, breaking, even while there pierced through my sense of ruin a prodigious private triumph, into breathless reasurance.

"She isn't there, little lady, and nobody's there—and you never see nothing, my sweet! How can poor Miss Jessel? when poor Miss Jessel's dead and buried? *We* know, don't we, love?"—and she appealed, blundering in, to the child. "It's all a mere mistake and a worry and a joke—and we'll go home as fast as we can!"

Our companion, on this, had responded with a strange, quick primness of propriety, and they were again, with Mrs. Grose on her feet, united, as it were, in pained opposition to me. Flora continued to fix me with her small mask of reprobation, and even at that minute I prayed God to forgive me for seeming to see that, as she stood there holding tight to our friend's dress, her incomparable childish beauty had suddenly failed, had quite vanished. I've said it already—she was literally, she was hideously, hard; she had turned common and almost ugly. "I don't know what you mean. I see nobody. I see nothing. I never *have.* I think you're cruel. I don't like you!" Then, after this deliverance, which might have been that of a vulgarly pert little girl in the street, she hugged Mrs. Grose more closely and buried in her skirts the dreadful little face. In this position she produced an almost furious wail. "Take me away, take me away—oh, take me away from *her!*"

"From *me?*" I panted.

"From you—from you!" she cried.

Even Mrs. Grose looked across at me dismayed, while I had nothing to do but communicate again with the figure that, on the opposite bank, without a movement, as rigidly still as if catching, beyond the interval, our voices, was as vividly there for my disaster as it was not there for my service. The wretched child had spoken exactly as if she had got from some outside source each of her stabbing little words, and I could therefore, in the full despair of all I had to accept, but sadly shake my head at her. "If I had ever doubted, all my doubt would at present have gone. I've been living with the miserable truth, and now it has only too much closed round me. Of course I've lost you: I've interfered, and you've seen—under *her* dictation"—with which I faced, over the pool again, our infernal witness—"the easy and perfect way to meet it. I've done my best, but I've lost you. Good-bye." For Mrs. Grose I had an imperative, an almost frantic "Go, go!" before which, in infinite distress, but mutely possessed of the little girl and clearly convinced, in spite of her blindness, that something awful had occurred and some collapse engulfed us, she retreated, by the way we had come, as fast as she could move.

Of what first happened when I was left alone I had no subsequent memory. I only knew that at the end of, I suppose, a quarter of an hour, an odorous dampness and roughness, chilling and piercing my trouble, had made me understand that I must have thrown myself, on my face, on the ground and given way to a wildness of grief. I must have lain there long and cried and sobbed, for when I raised my head the day was almost done. I got up and looked a moment, through the twilight, at the grey pool and its blank, haunted edge, and then I took, back to the house, my dreary and difficult course. When I reached the gate in the fence the boat, to my surprise, was gone, so that I had a fresh reflection to make on Flora's extraordinary command of the situation. She passed that night, by the most tacit, and I should add, were not the word so grotesque a false note, the happiest of arrangements, with Mrs. Grose. I saw neither of them on my return, but, on the other hand as by an ambiguous compensation, I saw a great deal of Miles. I saw—I can use no other phrase—so much of him that it was as if it were more than it had ever been. No evening I had passed at Bly had the portentous quality of this one; in spite of which —and in spite also of the deeper depths of consternation that had opened beneath my feet—there was literally, in the ebbing actual, an extraordinarily sweet sadness. On reaching the house I had never so much as looked for the boy; I had simply gone straight to my room to change what I was wearing and to take in, at a glance, much material testimony to Flora's rupture. Her little belongings had all been removed. When later, by the schoolroom fire, I was served with tea by the usual maid, I indulged, on the article of my other pupil, in no inquiry whatever. He had his freedom now—he might have it to the end! Well, he did have it; and it consisted—in part at least— of his coming in at about eight o'clock and sitting down with me in silence. On the removal of the tea-things I had blown out the candles and drawn my chair closer: I was conscious of a mortal coldness and felt as if I should never again be warm. So, when he appeared, I was sitting in the glow with my thoughts. He paused a moment by the door as if to look at me; then—as if to share them —came to the other side of the hearth and sank into a chair. We sat there in absolute stillness; yet he wanted, I felt, to be with me.

XXI

BEFORE a new day, in my room, had fully broken, my eyes opened to Mrs. Grose, who had come to my bedside with worse news. Flora was so markedly feverish that an illness was perhaps at hand; she had passed a night of extreme unrest, a night agitated above all by fears that had for their subject not in the least her former, but wholly her present, governess. It was not against the possible re-entrance of Miss Jessel on the scene that she protested—it was conspicuously and passionately against mine. I was promptly on my feet of course, and with an immense deal to ask; the more that my friend had discernibly now girded her loins to meet me once more. This I felt as soon as I had put to her the question of her sense of the child's sincerity as against my own. "She persists in denying to you that she saw, or has ever seen, anything?"

My visitor's trouble, truly, was great. "Ah, Miss it isn't a matter on which I can push her! Yet it isn't either, I must say, as if I much needed to. It has made her, every inch of her, quite old."

"Oh, I see her prefectly from here. She resents, for all the world like some high little personage, the imputation on her truthfulness and, as it were, her respectability. 'Miss Jessel indeed—*she!*' Ah, she's 'respectable,' the chit! The impression she gave me there yesterday was, I assure you, the very strangest of all; it was quite beyond any of the others. I *did* put my foot in it! She'll never speak to me again."

Hideous and obscure as it all was, it held Mrs. Grose briefly silent; then she granted my point with a frankness which, I made sure, had more behind it. "I think indeed, Miss, she never will. She do have a grand manner about it!"

"And that manner"—I summed it up—"is practically what's the matter with her now!"

Oh, that manner, I could see in my visitor's face, and not a little else besides! "She asks me every three minutes if I think you're coming in."

"I see—I see." I too, on my side, had so much more than worked it out. "Has she said to you since yesterday —except to repudiate her familiarity with anything so dreadful—a single other word about Miss Jessel?"

"Not one, Miss. And of course you know," my friend added, "I took it from her, by the lake, that, just then and there at least, there *was* nobody."

"Rather! And, naturally, you take it from her still."

"I don't contradict her. What else can I do?"

"Nothing in the world! You've the cleverest little person to deal with. They've made them—their two friends, I mean—still cleverer even than nature did; for it was wondrous material to play on! Flora has now her grievance, and she'll work it to the end."

"Yes, Miss; but to *what* end?"

"Why, that of dealing with me to her uncle. She'll make me out to him the lowest creature——!"

I winced at the fair show of the scene in Mrs. Grose's face: she looked for a minute as if she sharply saw them together. "And him who thinks so well of you!"

"He has an odd way—it comes over me now," I laughed, "—of proving it! But that doesn't matter. What Flora wants, of course, is to get rid of me."

My companion bravely concurred. "Never again to so much as look at you."

"So that what you've come to me now for," I asked, "is to speed me on my way?" Before she had time to reply, however, I had her in check. "I've a better idea—the result of my reflections. My going *would* seem the right thing, and on Sunday I was terribly near it. Yet that won't do. It's *you* who must go. You must take Flora."

My visitor, at this, did speculate. "But where in the world——?"

"Away from here. Away from *them*. Away, even most of all, now, from me. Straight to her uncle."

"Only to tell on you——?"

"No, not 'only'! To leave me, in addition, with my remedy."

She was still vague. "And what *is* your remedy?"

"Your loyalty, to begin with. And then Miles's."

She looked at me hard. "Do you think he——?"

"Won't if he has the chance, turn on me? Yes, I venture still to think it. At all events, I want to try. Get off with his sister as soon as possible and leave me with him alone." I was amazed, myself, at the spirit I had still in reserve, and therefore perhaps a trifle the more disconcerted at the way in which, in spite of this fine example of it, she hesitated. "There's one thing, of course," I went on: "they mustn't, before she goes, see each other for three seconds." Then it came over me that, in spite of Flora's presumable sequestration from the instant of her return from the pool, it might already be too late. "Do you mean," I anxiously asked, "that they *have* met?"

At this she quite flushed. "Ah, Miss, I'm not such a fool as that! If I've been obliged to leave her three or four times, it has been each time with one of the maids, and at present, though she's alone, she's locked in safe. And yet—and yet!" There were too many things.

"And yet what?"

"Well, are you so sure of the little gentleman?"

"I'm not sure of anything but *you*. But I have, since last evening, a new hope. I think he wants to give me an opening. I do believe that—poor little exquisite wretch! —he wants to speak. Last evening, in the firelight and the silence, he sat with me for two hours as if it were just coming."

Mrs. Grose looked hard, through the window, at the grey, gathering day. "And did it come?"

"No, though I waited and waited, I confess it didn't, and it was without a breach of the silence or so much as a faint allusion to his sister's condition and absence that we at last kissed for good-night. All the same," I continued, "I can't, if her uncle sees her, consent to his seeing her brother without my having given the boy—and most of all because things have got so bad—a little more time."

My friend appeared on this ground more reluctant than I could quite understand. "What do you mean by more time?"

"Well, a day or two—really to bring it out. He'll then be on *my* side—of which you see the importance. If nothing comes, I shall only fail, and you will, at the worst, have helped me by doing, on your arrival in town, whatever you may have found possible." So I put it before her, but she continued for a little so inscrutably embarrassed that I came again to her aid. "Unless, indeed," I wound up, "you really want *not* to go."

I could see it, in her face, at last clear itself; she put out her hand to me as a pledge. "I'll go—I'll go. I'll go this morning."

I wanted to be very just. "If you *should* wish still to wait, I would engage she shouldn't see me."

"No, no: it's the place itself. She must leave it." She held me a moment with heavy eyes, then brought out the rest. "Your idea's the right one. I myself, Miss——"

"Well?"

"I can't stay."

The look she gave me with it made me jump at possibilities. "You mean that, since yesterday, you *have* seen——?"

She shook her head with dignity. "I've *heard*——!"

"Heard?"

"From that child—horrors! There!" she sighed with tragic relief. "On my honour, Miss, she says things——!"

But at this evocation she broke down; she dropped, with a sudden sob, upon my sofa and, as I had seen her do before, gave way to all the grief of it.

It was quite in another manner that I, for my part, let myself go. "Oh, thank God!"

She sprang up again at this, drying her eyes with a groan. "'Thank God'?"

"It so justifies me!"

"It does that, Miss!"

I couldn't have desired more emphasis, but I just hesitated. "She's so horrible?"

I saw my colleague scarce knew how to put it. "Really shocking."

"And about me?"

"About you, Miss—since you must have it. It's beyond everything, for a young lady; and I can't think wherever she must have picked up——"

"The appalling language she applied to me? I can, then!" I broke in with a laugh that was doubtless significant enough.

It only, in truth, left my friend still more grave. "Well, perhaps I ought to also—since I've heard some of it before! Yet I can't bear it," the poor woman went on while, with the same movement, she glanced, on my dressing-table, at the face of my watch. "But I must go back."

I kept her, however. "Ah, if you can't bear it——!"

"How can I stop with her, you mean? Why, just for that: to get her away. Far from this," she pursued, "far from them——"

"She may be different? she may be free?" I seized her almost with joy. "Then, in spite of yesterday, you believe——"

"In such doings?" Her simple description of them required, in the light of her expression, to be carried no further, and she gave me the whole thing as she had never done. "I believe."

Yes, it was a joy, and we were still shoulder to shoulder:

if I might continue sure of that I should care but little what else happened. My support in the presence of disaster would be the same as it had been in my early need of confidence, and if my friend would answer for my honesty, I would answer for all the rest. On the point of taking leave of her, none the less, I was to some extent embarrassed. "There's one thing of course—it occurs to me—to remember. My letter, giving the alarm, will have reached town before you."

I now perceived still more how she had been beating about the bush and how weary at last it had made her. "Your letter won't have got there. Your letter never went."

"What then became of it?"

"Goodness knows! Master Miles——"

"Do you mean *he* took it?" I gasped.

She hung fire, but she overcame her reluctance. "I mean that I saw yesterday, when I came back with Miss Flora, that it wasn't where you had put it. Later in the evening I had the chance to question Luke, and he declared that he had neither noticed nor touched it." We could only exchange, on this, one of our deeper mutual soundings, and it was Mrs. Grose who first brought up the plumb with an almost elate "You see!"

"Yes, I see that if Miles took it instead he probably will have read it and destroyed it."

"And don't you see anything else?"

I faced her a moment with a sad smile. "It strikes me that by this time your eyes are open even wider than mine."

They proved to be so indeed, but she could still blush, almost, to show it. "I make out now what he must have done at school." And she gave, in her simple sharpness, an almost droll disillusioned nod. "He stole!"

I turned it over—I tried to be more judicial. "Well—perhaps."

She looked as if she found me unexpectedly calm. "He stole *letters!*"

She couldn't know my reasons for a calmness after all pretty shallow; so I showed them off as I might. "I hope then it was to more purpose than in this case! The note, at any rate, that I put on the table yesterday," I pursued, "will have given him so scant an advantage—for it contained only the bare demand for an interview—that he is already much ashamed of having gone so far for so little, and that what he had on his mind last evening was precisely the need of confession." I seemed to myself, for the instant, to have mastered it, to see it all. "Leave us, leave us"—I was already, at the door, hurrying her off. "I'll get it out of him. He'll meet me—he'll confess. If he confesses, he's saved. And if he's saved——"

"Then *you* are?" The dear woman kissed me on this, and I took her farewell. "I'll save you without him!" she cried as she went.

XXII

YET it was when she had got off—and I missed her on the spot—that the great pinch really came. If I had counted on what it would give me to find myself alone with Miles, I speedily perceived, at least, that it would give me a measure. No hour of my stay in fact was so assailed with apprehensions as that of my coming down to learn that the carriage containing Mrs. Grose and my younger pupil had already rolled out of the gates. Now I *was*, I said to myself, face to face with the elements, and for much of the rest of the day, while I fought my weakness, I could consider that I had been supremely rash. It was a tighter place still than I had yet turned round in; all the more that, for the first time, I could see in the aspect of others a confused reflection of the crisis. What had happened naturally caused them all to stare; there was too little of the explained, throw out whatever we might, in the suddenness of my colleague's act. The maids and the men looked blank; the effect of which on my nerves was an aggravation until I saw the necessity of making it a positive aid. It was precisely, in short, by just clutching the helm that I avoided total wreck; and I dare say that, to bear up at all, I became, that morning, very grand and very dry. I welcomed the consciousness that I was charged with much to do, and I caused it to be known as well that, left thus to myself, I was quite remarkably firm. I wandered with that manner, for the next hour or two, all over the place and looked, I have no doubt, as if I were ready for any onset. So, for the benefit of whom it might concern, I paraded with a sick heart.

The person it appeared least to concern proved to be, till dinner, little Miles himself. My perambulations had given me meanwhile, no glimpse of him, but they had tended to make more public the change taking place in our relation as a consequence of his having at the piano, the day before, kept me, in Flora's interest, so beguiled and befooled. The stamp of publicity had of course been fully given by her confinement and departure, and the change itself was now ushered in by our non-observance of the regular custom of the schoolroom. He had already disappeared when, on my way down, I pushed open his door, and I learned below that he had breakfasted—in the presence of a couple of the maids—with Mrs. Grose and his sister. He had then gone out, as he said, for a stroll; than which nothing, I reflected, could better have expressed his frank view of the abrupt transformation of my office. What he would now permit this office to consist of was yet to be settled: there was a queer relief, at all events—I mean for myself in especial—in the renouncement of one pretension. If so much had sprung to the surface, I scarce put it too strongly in saying that what had perhaps sprung highest was the absurdity of our prolonging the fiction that I had anything more to teach him. It sufficiently stuck out that, by tacit little tricks in which even more than myself he carried out the care for my dignity, I had had to appeal to him to let me off straining to meet him on the ground of his true capacity. He had at any rate his freedom now; I was never to touch it again; as I had amply shown, moreover, when, on his joining me in the schoolroom the previous night, I had uttered, on the subject of the interval just concluded, neither challenge nor hint. I had too much, from this moment, my other ideas. Yet when he at last arrived the difficulty of applying them, the accumulations of my problem, were brought straight home to me by the beautiful little presence on which what had occurred had as yet, for the eye, dropped neither stain nor shadow.

To mark, for the house, the high state I cultivated I decreed that my meals with the boy should be served, as we called it, downstairs; so that I had been awaiting him

in the ponderous pomp of the room outside of the window
of which I had had from Mrs. Grose, that first scared
Sunday, my flash of something it would scarce have done
to call light. Here at present I felt afresh—for I had felt
it again and again—how my equilibrium depended on the
success of my rigid will, the will to shut my eyes as tight
as possible to the truth that what I had to deal with was,
revoltingly, against nature. I could only get on at all by
taking "nature" into my confidence and my account, by
treating my monstrous ordeal as a push in a direction
unusual, of course, and unpleasant, but demanding, after
all, for a fair front, only another turn of the screw of
ordinary human virtue. No attempt, none the less, could
well require more tact than just this attempt to supply,
one's self, *all* the nature. How could I put even a little of
that article into a suppression of reference to what had
occurred? How, on the other hand, could I make a reference without a new plunge into the hideous obscure?
Well, a sort of answer, after a time, had come to me, and
it was so far confirmed as that I was met, incontestably,
by the quickened vision of what was rare in my little companion. It was indeed as if he had found even now—as
he had so often found at lessons—still some other delicate
way to ease me off. Wasn't there light in the fact which,
as we shared our solitude, broke out with a specious glitter
it had never yet quite worn?—the fact that (opportunity
aiding, precious opportunity which had now come) it
would be preposterous, with a child so endowed, to forgo
the help one might wrest from absolute intelligence? What
had his intelligence been given him for but to save him?
Mightn't one, to reach his mind, risk the stretch of an
angular arm over his character? It was as if, when we were
face to face in the dining-room, he had literally shown me
the way. The roast mutton was on the table, and I had
dispensed with attendance. Miles, before he sat down,
stood a moment with his hands in his pockets and looked
at the joint, on which he seemed on the point of passing

some humorous judgment. But what he presently produced was: "I say, my dear, is she really very awfully ill?"

"Little Flora? Not so bad but that she'll presently be better. London will set her up. Bly had ceased to agree with her. Come here and take your mutton."

He alertly obeyed me, carried the plate carefully to his seat, and, when he was established, went on. "Did Bly disagree with her so terribly suddenly?"

"Not so suddenly as you might think. One had seen it coming on."

"Then why didn't you get her off before?"

"Before what?"

"Before she became too ill to travel."

I found myself prompt. "She's *not* too ill to travel: she only might have become so if she had stayed. This was just the moment to seize. The journey will dissipate the influence"—oh, I was grand!—"and carry it off."

"I see, I see"—Miles, for that matter, was grand too. He settled to his repast with the charming little "table manner" that, from the day of his arrival, had relieved me of all grossness of admonition. Whatever he had been driven from school for, it was not for ugly feeding. He was irreproachable, as always, today; but he was unmistakeably more conscious. He was discernibly trying to take for granted more things than he found, without assistance, quite easy; and he dropped into peaceful silence while he felt his situation. Our meal was of the briefest—mine a vain pretence, and I had the things immediately removed. While this was done Miles stood again with his hands in his little pockets and his back to me—stood and looked out of the wide window through which, that other day, I had seen what pulled me up. We continued silent while the maid was with us—as silent, it whimsically occurred to me, as some young couple who, on their wedding-journey, at the inn, feel shy in the presence of the waiter. He turned round only when the waiter had left us. "Well—so we're alone!"

XXIII

"Oh, more or less." I fancy my smile was pale. "Not absolutely. We shouldn't like that!" I went on.

"No—I suppose we shouldn't. Of course we have the others."

"We have the others—we have indeed the others," I concurred.

"Yet even though we have them," he returned, still with his hands in his pockets and planted there in front of me, "they don't much count, do they?"

I made the best of it, but I felt wan. "It depends on what you call 'much'!"

"Yes"— with all accommodation — "everything depends!" On this, however, he faced to the window again and presently reached it with his vague, restless, cogitating step. He remained there awhile, with his forehead against the glass, in contemplation of the stupid shrubs I knew and the dull things of November. I had always my hypocrisy of "work," behind which, now, I gained the sofa. Steadying myself with it there as I had repeatedly done at those moments of torment that I have described as the moments of my knowing the children to be given to something from which I was barred, I sufficiently obeyed my habit of being prepared for the worst. But an extraordinary impression dropped on me as I extracted a meaning from the boy's embarrassed back—none other than the impression that I was not barred now. This inference grew in a few minutes to sharp intensity and seemed bound up with the direct perception that it was positively *he* who was. The frames and squares of the great window were a kind of image, for him, of a kind of failure. I felt that I saw him, at any rate, shut in or shut out. He was admirable, but not comfortable: I took it in with a throb of hope. Wasn't he looking, through the haunted pane, for something he couldn't see?—and wasn't it the first time in the whole business that he had known such a lapse? The first, the very first: I found it a splendid portent. It made him anxious, though he watched himself; he had been anxious all day and, even while in his usual sweet little manner he sat at table, had needed all his small strange genius to give it a gloss. When he at last turned round to meet me, it was almost as if this genius had succumbed. "Well, I think I'm glad Bly agrees with *me!*"

"You would certainly seem to have seen, these twenty-four hours, a good deal more of it than for some time before. I hope," I went on bravely, "that you've been enjoying yourself."

"Oh, yes, I've been ever so far; all round about—miles and miles away. I've never been so free."

He had really a manner of his own, and I could only try to keep up with him. "Well, do you like it?"

He stood there smiling; then at last he put into two words—"Do *you?*"—more discrimination than I had ever heard two words contain. Before I had time to deal with that, however, he continued as if with the sense that this was an impertinence to be softened. "Nothing could be more charming than the way you take it, for of course if we're alone together now it's you that are alone most. But I hope," he threw in, "you don't particularly mind!"

"Having to do with you?" I asked. "My dear child, how can I help minding? Though I've renounced all claim to your company,—you're so beyond me,—I at least greatly enjoy it. What else should I stay on for?"

He looked at me more directly, and the expression of his face, graver now, struck me as the most beautiful I had ever found in it. "You stay on just for *that?*"

"Certainly. I stay on as your friend and from the tremendous interest I take in you till something can be done for you that may be more worth your while. That needn't surprise you." My voice trembled so that I felt it impossible to suppress the shake. "Don't you remember how I told you, when I came and sat on your bed the night of the storm, that there was nothing in the world I wouldn't do for you?"

"Yes, yes!" He, on his side, more and more visibly nervous, had a tone to master; but he was so much more successful than I that, laughing out through his gravity, he could pretend we were pleasantly jesting. "Only that, I think, was to get me to do something for *you!*"

"It was partly to get you to do something," I conceded. "But, you know, you didn't do it."

"Oh, yes," he said with the brightest superficial eagerness, "you wanted me to tell you something."

"That's it. Out, straight out. What you have on your mind, you know."

"Ah, then, is *that* what you've stayed over for?"

He spoke with a gaiety through which I could still catch the finest little quiver of resentful passion; but I can't begin to express the effect upon me of an implication of surrender even so faint. It was as if what I had yearned for had come at last only to astonish me. "Well, yes— I may as well make a clean breast of it. It was precisely for that."

He waited so long that I supposed it for the purpose of repudiating the assumption on which my action had been founded; but what he finally said was: "Do you mean now—here?"

"There couldn't be a better place or time." He looked round him uneasily, and I had the rare—oh, the queer!— impression of the very first symptom I had seen in him of the approach of immediate fear. It was as if he were suddenly afraid of me—which struck me indeed as perhaps the best thing to make him. Yet in the very pang of the effort I felt it vain to try sternness, and I heard myself the next instant so gentle as to be almost grotesque. "You want so to go out again?"

"Awfully!" He smiled at me heroically, and the touch‑ing little bravery of it was enhanced by his actually flushing with pain. He had picked up his hat, which he had brought in, and stood twirling it in a way that gave me, even as I was just nearly reaching port, a perverse horror of what I was doing. To do it in *any* way was an act of violence, for what did it consist of but the obtrusion of the idea of grossness and guilt on a small helpless crea‑ture who had been for me a revelation of the possibilities of beautiful intercourse? Wasn't it base to create for a being so exquisite a mere alien awkwardness? I suppose I now read into our situation a clearness it couldn't have had at the time, for I seem to see our poor eyes already lighted with some spark of a prevision of the anguish that was to come. So we circled about, with terrors and scruples, like fighters not daring to close. But it was for each other we feared! That kept us a little longer sus‑pended and unbruised. "I'll tell you everything," Miles said—"I mean I'll tell you anything you like. You'll stay on with me, and we shall both be all right and I *will* tell you—I *will*. But not now."

"Why not now?"

My insistence turned him from me and kept him once more at his window in a silence during which, between us, you might have heard a pin drop. Then he was before me again with the air of a person for whom, outside, someone who had frankly to be reckoned with was waiting. "I have to see Luke."

I had not yet reduced him to quite so vulgar a lie, and I felt proportionately ashamed. But, horrible as it was, his lies made up my truth. I achieved thoughtfully a few loops of my knitting. "Well, then, go to Luke, and I'll wait for what you promise. Only, in return for that, satisfy, before you leave me, one very much smaller request."

He looked as if he felt he had succeeded enough to be

able still a little to bargain. "Very much smaller——?"

"Yes, a mere fraction of the whole. Tell me"—oh, my work preoccupied me, and I was off-hand!—"if, yesterday afternoon, from the table in the hall, you took, you know, my letter."

XXIV

My sense of how he received this suffered for a minute from something that I can describe only as a fierce split of my attention—a stroke that at first, as I sprang straight up, reduced me to the mere blind movement of getting hold of him, drawing him close, and, while I just fell for support against the nearest piece of furniture, instinctively keeping him with his back to the window. The appearance was full upon us that I had already had to deal with here: Peter Quint had come into view like a sentinel before a prison. The next thing I saw was that, from outside, he had reached the window, and then I knew that, close to the glass and glaring in through it, he offered once more to the room his white face of damnation. It represents but grossly what took place within me at the sight to say that on the second my decision was made; yet I believe that no woman so overwhelmed ever in so short a time recovered her grasp of the *act*. It came to me in the very horror of the immediate presence that the act would be, seeing and facing what I saw and faced, to keep the boy himself unaware. The inspiration—I can call it by no other name—was that I felt how voluntarily, how transcendently, I *might*. It was like fighting with a demon for a human soul, and when I had fairly so appraised it I saw how the human soul—held out, in the tremor of my hands, at arm's length—had a perfect dew of sweat on a lovely childish forehead. The face that was close to mine was as white as the face against the glass, and out of it presently came a sound, not low nor weak, but as if from much further away, that I drank like a waft of fragrance.

"Yes—I took it."

At this, with a moan of joy, I enfolded, I drew him close; and while I held him to my breast, where I could feel in the sudden fever of his little body the tremendous pulse of his little heart, I kept my eyes on the thing at the window and saw it move and shift its posture. I have likened it to a sentinel, but its slow wheel, for a moment, was rather the prowl of a baffled beast. My present quickened courage, however, was such that, not too much to let it through, I had to shade, as it were, my flame. Meanwhile the glare of the face was again at the window, the scoundrel fixed as if to watch and wait. It was the very confidence that I might now defy him, as well as the positive certitude, by this time, of the child's unconsciousness, that made me go on. "What did you take it for?"

"To see what you said about me."

"You opened the letter?"

"I opened it."

My eyes were now, as I held him off a little again, on Miles's own face, in which the collapse of mockery showed me how complete was the ravage of uneasiness. What was prodigious was that at last, by my success, his sense was sealed and his communication stopped: he knew that he was in presence, but knew not of what, and knew still less that I also was and that I did know. And what did this strain of trouble matter when my eyes went back to the window only to see that the air was clear again and—by my personal triumph—the influence quenched? There was nothing there. I felt that the cause was mine and that I should surely get *all*. "And you found nothing!"—I let my elation out.

He gave the most mournful, thoughtful little head-shake. "Nothing."

"Nothing, nothing!" I almost shouted in my joy.

"Nothing, nothing," he sadly repeated.

I kissed his forehead; it was drenched. "So what have you done with it?"

"I've burnt it."

"Burnt it?" It was now or never. "Is that what you did at school?"

Oh, what this brought up! "At school?"

"Did you take letters?—or other things?"

"Other things?" He appeared now to be thinking of something far off and that reached him only through the pressure of his anxiety. Yet it did reach him. "Did I *steal?*"

I felt myself redden to the roots of my hair as well as wonder if it were more strange to put to a gentleman such a question or to see him take it with allowances that gave the very distance of his fall in the world. "Was it for that you mightn't go back?"

The only thing he felt was rather a dreary little surprise. "Did you know I mightn't go back?"

"I know everything."

He gave me at this the longest and strangest look. "Everything?"

"Everything. Therefore *did* you——?" But I couldn't say it again.

Miles could, very simply. "No. I didn't steal."

My face must have shown him I believed him utterly; yet my hands—but it was for pure tenderness—shook him as if to ask him why, if it was all for nothing, he had condemned me to months of torment. "What then did you do?"

He looked in vague pain all round the top of the room and drew his breath, two or three times over, as if with difficulty. He might have been standing at the bottom of the sea and raising his eyes to some faint green twilight. "Well—I said things."

"Only that?"

"They thought it was enough!"

"To turn you out for?"

Never, truly, had a person "turned out" shown so little to explain it as this little person! He appeared to weigh my question, but in a manner quite detached and almost helpless. "Well, I suppose I oughtn't."

"But to whom did you say them?"

He evidently tried to remember, but it dropped—he had lost it. "I don't know!"

He almost smiled at me in the desolation of his surrender, which was indeed practically, by this time, so complete that I ought to have left it there. But I was infatuated—I was blind with victory, though even then the very effect that was to have brought him so much nearer was already that of added separation. "Was it to everyone?" I asked.

"No; it was only to——" But he gave a sick little headshake. "I don't remember their names."

"Were they then so many?"

"No—only a few. Those I liked."

Those he liked? I seemed to float not into clearness, but into a darker obscure, and within a minute there had come to me out of my very pity the appalling alarm of his being perhaps innocent. It was for the instant confounding and bottomless, for if he *were* innocent, what then on earth was *I*? Paralysed, while it lasted, by the mere brush of the question, I let him go a little, so that, with a deep-drawn sigh, he turned away from me again; which, as he faced toward the clear window, I suffered, feeling that I had nothing now there to keep him from. "And did they repeat what you said?" I went on after a moment.

He was soon at some distance from me, still breathing hard and again with the air, though now without anger for it, of being confined against his will. Once more, as he had done before, he looked up at the dim day as if, of what had hitherto sustained him, nothing was left but an unspeakable anxiety. "Oh, yes," he nevertheless replied—"they must have repeated them. To those *they* liked," he added.

There was, somehow, less of it than I had expected; but

I turned it over. "And these things came round——?"

"To the masters? Oh, yes!" he answered very simply. "But I didn't know they'd tell."

"The masters? They didn't—they've never told. That's why I ask you."

He turned to me again his little beautiful fevered face. "Yes, it was too bad."

"Too bad?"

"What I suppose I sometimes said. To write home."

I can't name the exquisite pathos of the contradiction given to such a speech by such a speaker; I only know that the next instant I heard myself throw off with homely force: "Stuff and nonsense!" But the next after that I must have sounded stern enough. "What were these things?"

My sternness was all for his judge, his executioner; yet it made him avert himself again, and that movement made *me*, with a single bound and an irrepressible cry, spring straight upon him. For there again, against the glass, as if to blight his confession and stay his answer, was the hideous author of our woe—the white face of damnation. I felt a sick swim at the drop of my victory and all the return of my battle, so that the wildness of my veritable leap only served as a great betrayal. I saw him, from the midst of my act, meet it with a divination, and on the perception that even now he only guessed, and that the window was still to his own eyes free, I let the impulse flame up to convert the climax of his dismay into the very proof of his liberation. "No more, no more, no more!" I shrieked, as I tried to press him against me, to my visitant.

"Is she *here*?" Miles panted as he caught with his sealed eyes the direction of my words. Then as his strange "she" staggered me and, with a gasp, I echoed it, "Miss Jessel, Miss Jessel!" he with a sudden fury gave me back.

I seized, stupefied, his supposition—some sequel to what we had done to Flora, but this made me only want to show him that it was better still than that. "It's not

Miss Jessel! But it's at the window—straight before us. It's *there*—the coward horror, there for the last time!"

At this, after a second in which his head made the movement of a baffled dog's on a scent and then gave a frantic little shake for air and light, he was at me in a white rage, bewildered, glaring vainly over the place and missing wholly, though it now, to my sense, filled the room like the taste of poison, the wide, overwhelming presence. "It's *he*?"

I was so determined to have all my proof that I flashed into ice to challenge him. "Whom do you mean by 'he'?"

"Peter Quint—you devil!" His face gave again, round the room, its convulsed supplication. "*Where*?"

They are in my ears still, his supreme surrender of the name and his tribute to my devotion. "What does he matter now, my own?—what will he *ever* matter? *I* have you," I launched at the beast, "but he has lost you for ever!" Then, for the demonstration of my work, "There, *there*!" I said to Miles.

But he had already jerked straight round, stared, glared again, and seen but the quiet day. With the stroke of the loss I was so proud of he uttered the cry of a creature hurled over an abyss, and the grasp with which I recovered him might have been that of catching him in his fall. I caught him, yes, I held him—it may be imagined with what a passion; but at the end of a minute I began to feel what it truly was that I held. We were alone with the quiet day, and his little heart, dispossessed, had stopped.

THE LESSON OF THE MASTER

THE LESSON OF THE MASTER

I

He had been told the ladies were at church, but this
was corrected by what he saw from the top of the steps—
they descended from a great height in two arms, with a cir-
cular sweep of the most charming effect—at the threshold
of the door which, from the long bright gallery, overlooked
the immense lawn. Three gentlemen, on the grass, at a
distance, sat under the great trees, while the fourth figure
showed a crimson dress that told as a "bit of colour"
amid the fresh rich green. The servant had so far accompanied Paul Overt as to introduce him to this view, after
asking him if he wished first to go to his room. The young
man declined that privilege, conscious of no disrepair from
so short and easy a journey and always liking to take at
once a general perceptive possession of a new scene. He
stood there a little with his eyes on the group and on the
admirable picture, the wide grounds of an old country-
house near London—that only made it better—on a splendid Sunday in June. "But that lady, who's *she?*" he said
to the servant before the man left him.

"I think she's Mrs. St. George, sir."

"Mrs. St. George the wife of the distinguished—" Then
Paul Overt checked himself, doubting if a footman would
know.

"Yes, sir—probably, sir," said his guide, who appeared
to wish to intimate that a person staying at Summersoft
would naturally be, if only by alliance, distinguished.
His tone, however, made poor Overt himself feel for the
moment scantly so.

"And the gentlemen?" Overt went on.

"Well, sir, one of them's General Fancourt."

"Ah yes, I know; thank you." General Fancourt was distinguished, there was no doubt of that, for something he had done, or perhaps even hadn't done—the young man couldn't remember which—some years before in India. The servant went away, leaving the glass doors open into the gallery, and Paul Overt remained at the head of the wide double staircase, saying to himself that the place was sweet and promised a pleasant visit, while he leaned on the balustrade of fine old ironwork which, like all the other details, was of the same period as the house. It all went together and spoke in one voice—a rich English voice of the early part of the eighteenth century. It might have been church-time on a summer's day in the reign of Queen Anne: the stillness was too perfect to be modern, the nearness counted so as distance, and there was something so fresh and sound in the originality of the large smooth house, the expanse of beautiful brick-work that showed for pink rather than red and that had been kept clear of messy creepers by the law under which a woman with a rare complexion disdains a veil. When Paul Overt became aware that the people under the trees had noticed him he turned back through the open doors into the great gallery which was the pride of the place. It marched across from end to end and seemed—with its bright colours, its high panelled windows, its faded flow-ered chintzes, its quickly-recognised portraits and pic-tures, the blue-and-white china of its cabinets and the attenuated festoons and rosettes of its ceiling—a cheerful upholstered avenue into the other century.

Our friend was slightly nervous; that went with his character as a student of fine prose, went with the artist's general disposition to vibrate; and there was a particular thrill in the idea that Henry St. George might be a member of the party. For the young aspirant he had remained a high literary figure, in spite of the lower range of pro-duction to which he had fallen after his three first great

successes, the comparative absence of quality in his later
work. There had been moments when Paul Overt almost
shed tears for this; but now that he was near him—he had
never met him—he was conscious only of the fine original
source and of his own immense debt. After he had taken
a turn or two up and down the gallery he came out again
and descended the steps. He was but slenderly supplied
with a certain social boldness—it was really a weakness
in him—so that, conscious of a want of acquaintance with
the four persons in the distance, he gave way to motions
recommended by their not committing him to a positive
approach. There was a fine English awkwardness in this
—he felt that too as he sauntered vaguely and obliquely
across the lawn, taking an independent line. Fortunately
there was an equally fine English directness in the way
one of the gentlemen presently rose and made as if to
"stalk" him, though with an air of conciliation and reas-
surance. To this demonstration Paul Overt instantly responded, even if the gentleman were not his host. He was
tall, straight and elderly and had, like the great house
itself, a pink smiling face, and into the bargain a white
moustache. Our young man met him halfway while he
laughed and said: "Er—Lady Watermouth told us you
were coming; she asked me just to look after you." Paul
Overt thanked him, liking him on the spot, and turned
round with him to walk toward the others. "They've all
gone to church—all except us," the stranger continued
as they went; "we're just sitting here—it's so jolly."
Overt pronounced it jolly indeed: it was such a lovely
place. He mentioned that he was having the charming
impression for the first time.

"Ah you've not been here before?" said his companion.
"It's a nice little place—not much to *do,* you know."
Overt wondered what he wanted to "do"—he felt that he
himself was doing so much. By the time they came to
where the others sat he had recognised his initiator for a
military man and—such was the turn of Overt's imagina-

tion—had found him thus still more sympathetic. He would naturally have a need for action, for deeds at variance with the pacific pastoral scene. He was evidently so good-natured, however, that he accepted the inglorious hour for what it was worth. Paul Overt shared it with him and with his companions for the next twenty minutes; the latter looked at him and he looked at them without knowing much who they were, while the talk went on without much telling him even what it meant. It seemed indeed to mean nothing in particular; it wandered, with casual pointless pauses and short terrestrial flights, amid names of persons and places—names which, for our friend, had no great power of evocation. It was all sociable and slow, as was right and natural of a warm Sunday morning.

His first attention was given to the question, privately considered, of whether one of the two younger men would be Henry St. George. He knew many of his distinguished contemporaries by their photographs, but had never, as happened, seen a portrait of the great misguided novelist. One of the gentlemen was unimaginable—he was too young; and the other scarcely looked clever enough, with such mild undiscriminating eyes. If those eyes were St. George's the problem presented by the ill-matched parts of his genius would be still more difficult of solution. Besides, the deportment of their proprietor was not, as regards the lady in the red dress, such as could be natural, toward the wife of his bosom, even to a writer accused by several critics of sacrificing too much to manner. Lastly Paul Overt had a vague sense that if the gentleman with the expressionless eyes bore the name that had set his heart beating faster (he also had contradictory conventional whiskers—the young admirer of the celebrity had never in a mental vision seen *his* face in so vulgar a frame) he would have given him a sign of recognition or of friendliness, would have heard of him a little, would know something about "Ginistrella," would have an impression of how that fresh fiction had caught the eye of real criticism. Paul Overt had a dread of being grossly proud, but even morbid modesty might view the authorship of "Ginistrella" as constituting a degree of identity. His soldierly friend became clear enough: he was "Fancourt," but was also "the General"; and he mentioned to the new visitor in the course of a few moments that he had but lately returned from twenty years' service abroad.

"And now you remain in England?" the young man asked.

"Oh yes; I've bought a small house in London."

"And I hope you like it," said Overt, looking at Mrs. St. George.

"Well, a little house in Manchester Square—there's a limit to the enthusiasm *that* inspires."

"Oh I meant being at home again—being back in Piccadilly."

"My daughter likes Piccadilly—that's the main thing. She's very fond of art and music and literature and all that kind of thing. She missed it in India and she finds it in London, or she hopes she'll find it. Mr. St. George has promised to help her—he has been awfully kind to her. She has gone to church—she's fond of that too—but they'll all be back in a quarter of an hour. You must let me introduce you to her—she'll be so glad to know you. I dare say she has read every blest word you've written."

"I shall be delighted—I haven't written so very many," Overt pleaded, feeling, and without resentment, that the General at least was vagueness itself about that. But he wondered a little why, expressing this friendly disposition, it didn't occur to the doubtless eminent soldier to pronounce the word that would put him in relation with Mrs. St. George. If it was a question of introductions Miss Fancourt—apparently as yet unmarried—was far away, while the wife of his illustrious confrère was almost between them. This lady struck Paul Overt as altogether pretty, with a surprising juvenility and a high smartness of aspect, something that—he could scarcely have said why—served for mystification. St. George certainly had every right to a charming wife, but he himself would never have imagined the important little woman in the aggressively Parisian dress the partner for life, the *alter ego,* of a man of letters. That partner in general, he knew, that second self, was far from presenting herself in a single type: observation had taught him that she was not inveterately, not necessarily plain. But he had never before seen her look so much as if her prosperity had deeper foundations than an ink-spotted study-table littered with proof-sheets. Mrs. St. George might have been the wife of a gentleman who "kept" books rather than wrote them, who carried on great affairs in the City and made better bargains than those that poets mostly make with publishers. With this she hinted at a success more personal—a success peculiarly stamping the age in which society, the world of conversation, is a great drawing-room with the City for its antechamber. Overt numbered her years at first as some thirty, and then ended by believing that she might approach her fiftieth. But she somehow in this case juggled away the excess and the difference—you only saw them in a rare glimpse, like the rabbit in the conjuror's sleeve. She was extraordinarily white, and her every element and item was pretty; her eyes, her ears, her hair, her voice, her hands, her feet—to which her relaxed attitude in her wicker chair gave a great publicity—and the numerous ribbons and trinkets with which she was bedecked. She looked as if she had put on her best clothes to go to church and then had decided they were too good for that and had stayed at home. She told a story of some length about the shabby way Lady Jane had treated the Duchess, as well as an anecdote in relation to a purchase she had made in Paris—on her way back from Cannes; made for Lady Egbert, who had never refunded the money. Paul Overt suspected her of a tendency to figure great people as larger than life, until he noticed the manner in which she handled Lady Egbert, which was so sharply mutinous that it reassured him. He felt he should have understood her better if he might have met her eye; but she scarcely so much as glanced at him. "Ah here they come—all the good ones!" she said at last; and Paul Overt admired at his distance the return of the churchgoers—several persons, in couples and threes, advancing in a flicker of sun and shade at the end of a large green vista formed by the level grass and the overarching boughs.

"If you mean to imply that *we're* bad, I protest," said one of the gentlemen—"after making one's self agreeable all the morning!"

"Ah if they've found you agreeable—!" Mrs. St. George gaily cried. "But if we're good the others are better."

"They must be angels then," said the amused General

"Your husband was an angel, the way he went off at your bidding," the gentleman who had first spoken declared to Mrs. St. George.

"At my bidding?"

"Didn't you make him go to church?"

"I never made him do anything in my life but once—when I made him burn up a bad book. That's all!" At her "That's all!" our young friend broke into an irrepressible laugh; it lasted only a second, but it drew her eyes to him. His own met them, though not long enough to help him to understand her; unless it were a step toward this that he saw on the instant how the burnt book—the way she alluded to it!—would have been one of her husband's finest things.

"A bad book?" her interlocutor repeated.

"I didn't like it. He went to church because your daughter went," she continued to General Fancourt. "I think it my duty to call your attention to his extraordinary demonstrations to your daughter."

"Well, if you don't mind them I don't!" the General laughed.

"Il s'attache à ses pas. But I don't wonder—she's so charming."

"I hope she won't make him burn any books!" Paul Overt ventured to exclaim.

"If she'd make him write a few it would be more to the purpose," said Mrs. St. George. "He has been of a laziness of late—!"

Our young man stared—he was so struck with the lady's phraseology. Her "Write a few" seemed to him almost as good as her "That's all." Didn't she, as the wife of a rare artist, know what it was to produce *one* perfect work of art? How in the world did she think they were turned off? His private conviction was that, admirably as Henry St. George wrote, he had written for the last ten years, and especially for the last five, only too much, and there was an instant during which he felt inwardly solicited to make this public. But before he had spoken a diversion was effected by the return of the absentees. They strolled up dispersedly—there were eight or ten of them—and the circle under the trees rearranged itself as they took their place in it. They made it much larger, so that Paul Overt could feel—he was always feeling that sort of thing, as he said to himself—that if the company had already been interesting to watch the interest would now become intense. He shook hands with his hostess, who welcomed him without many words, in the manner of a woman able to trust him to understand and conscious that so pleasant an occasion would in every way speak for itself. She offered him no particular facility for sitting by her; when they had all subsided again he found himself still next General Fancourt, with an unknown lady on his other flank.

"That's my daughter—that one opposite," the General said to him without loss of time. Overt saw a tall girl, with magnificent red hair, in a dress of a pretty grey-green tint and of a limp silken texture, a garment that clearly shirked every modern effect. It had therefore some-how the stamp of the latest thing, so that our beholder quickly took her for nothing if not contemporaneous.

"She's very handsome—very handsome," he repeated while he considered her. There was something noble in her head, and she appeared fresh and strong.

Her good father surveyed her with complacency, remarking soon: "She looks too hot—that's her walk. But she'll be all right presently. Then I'll make her come over and speak to you."

"I should be sorry to give you that trouble. If you were to take me over *there*—!" the young man murmured.

"My dear sir, do you suppose I put myself out that way? I don't mean for you, but for Marian," the General added.

"*I* would put myself out for her soon enough," Overt replied; after which he went on: "Will you be so good as to tell me which of those gentlemen is Henry St. George?"

"The fellow talking to my girl. By Jove, he *is* making up to her—they're going off for another walk."

"Ah is that he—really?" Our friend felt a certain surprise, for the personage before him seemed to trouble a vision which had been vague only while not confronted with the reality. As soon as the reality dawned the mental image, retiring with a sigh, became substantial enough to suffer a slight wrong. Overt, who had spent a considerable part of his short life in foreign lands, made now, but not for the first time, the reflexion that whereas in those countries he had almost always recognised the artist and the man of letters by his personal "type," the mould of his face, the character of his head, the expression of his figure and even the indications of his dress, so in England this identification was as little as possible a matter of course, thanks to the greater conformity, the habit of sinking the profession instead of advertising it, the general diffusion of the air of the gentleman—the gentleman committed to no particular set of ideas. More than once, on returning to his own country, he had said to himself about people met in society: "One sees them in this place and that, and one even talks with them; but to find out what they *do* one would really have to be a detective." In respect to several individuals whose work he was the opposite of "drawn to"—perhaps he was wrong—he found himself adding "No wonder they conceal it—when it's so bad!" He noted that oftener than in France and in Germany his artist looked like a gentleman—that is like an English one—while, certainly outside a few exceptions, his gentleman didn't look like an artist. St. George was not one of the exceptions; that circumstance he definitely apprehended before the great man had turned his back to walk off with Miss Fancourt. He certainly looked better behind than any foreign man of letters—showed for beautifully correct in his tall black hat and his superior frock coat. Somehow, all the same, these very garments—he wouldn't have minded them so much on a week-day— were disconcerting to Paul Overt, who forgot for the moment that the head of the profession was not a bit better dressed than himself. He had caught a glimpse of a regular face, a fresh colour, a brown moustache and a pair of eyes surely never visited by a fine frenzy, and he promised himself to study these denotements on the first occasion. His superficial sense was that their owner might have passed for a lucky stockbroker—a gentleman driving eastward every morning from a sanitary suburb in a smart dog-cart. That carried out the impression already derived from his wife. Paul's glance, after a moment, travelled back to this lady, and he saw how her own had followed her husband as he moved off with Miss Fancourt. Overt permitted himself to wonder a little if she were jealous when another woman took him away. Then he made out that Mrs. St. George wasn't glaring at the indifferent maiden. Here eyes rested but on her husband, and with unmistakeable serenity. That was the way she wanted him to be—she liked his conventional uniform. Overt longed to hear more about the book she had induced him to destroy.

II

As they all came out from luncheon General Fancourt took hold of him with an "I say, I want you to know my girl!" as if the idea had just occurred to him and he hadn't spoken of it before. With the other hand he possessed himself all paternally of the young lady. "You know all about him. I've seen you with his books. She reads everything—everything!" he went on to Paul. The girl smiled at him and then laughed at her father. The General turned away and his daughter spoke—"Isn't papa delightful?"

"He is indeed, Miss Fancourt."

"As if I read you because I read 'everything'!"

"Oh I don't mean for saying that," said Paul Overt. "I liked him from the moment he began to be kind to me. Then he promised me this privilege."

"It isn't for you he means it—it's for me. If you flatter yourself that he thinks of anything in life but me you'll find you're mistaken. He introduces every one. He thinks me insatiable."

"You speak just like him," laughed our youth.

"Ah but sometimes I want to"—and the girl coloured. "I don't read everything—I read very little. But I *have* read you."

"Suppose we go into the gallery," said Paul Overt. She pleased him greatly, not so much because of this last remark—though that of course was not too disconcerting—as because, seated opposite to him at luncheon, she had given him for half an hour the impression of her beautiful face. Something else had come with it—a sense of generosity, of an enthusiasm which, unlike many enthusiasms, was not all manner. That was not spoiled for him by his seeing that the repast had placed her again in familiar contact with Henry St. George. Sitting next her this celebrity was also opposite our young man, who had been able to note that he multiplied the attentions lately brought by his wife to the General's notice. Paul Overt had gathered as well that this lady was not in the least discomposed by these fond excesses and that she gave every sign of an unclouded spirit. She had Lord Masham on one side of her and on the other the accomplished Mr. Mulliner, editor of the new high-class lively evening paper which was expected to meet a want felt in circles increasingly conscious that Conservatism must be made amusing, and unconvinced when assured by those of another political colour that it was already amusing enough. At the end of an hour spent in her company Paul Overt thought her still prettier than at the first radiation, and if her profane allusions to her husband's work had not still rung in his ears he should have liked her—so far as it could be a question of that in connexion with a woman to whom he had not yet spoken and to whom probably he should never speak if it were left to her. Pretty women were a clear need to this genius, and for the hour it was Miss Fancourt who supplied the want. If Overt had promised himself a closer view the occasion was now of the best, and it brought consequences felt by the young man as important. He saw more in St. George's face, which he liked the better for its not having told its whole story in the first three minutes. That story came out as one read, in short instalments—it was excusable that one's analogies should be somewhat professional—and the text was a style considerably involved, a language not easy to translate at sight. There were shades of meaning in it and a vague perspective of history which receded as you advanced. Two facts Paul had particularly heeded. The first of these was that he liked the measured mask much better at inscrutable rest than in social agitation; its almost convulsive smile above all displeased him (as much as any impression from that source could), whereas the quiet face had a charm that grew in proportion as stillness settled again. The change to the expression of gaiety excited, he made out, very much the private protest of a person sitting gratefully in the twilight when the lamp is brought in too soon. His second reflexion was that, though generally averse to the flagrant use of ingratiating arts by a man of age "making up" to a pretty girl, he was not in this case too painfully affected: which seemed to prove either that St. George had a light hand or the air of being younger than he was, or else that Miss Fancourt's own manner somehow made everything right.

Overt walked with her into the gallery, and they strolled to the end of it, looking at the pictures, the cabinets, the charming vista, which harmonised with the prospect of the summer afternoon, resembling it by a long brightness, with great divans and old chairs that figured hours of rest. Such a place as that had the added merit of giving those who came into it plenty to talk about. Miss Fancourt sat down with her new acquaintance on a flowered sofa, the cushions of which, very numerous, were tight ancient cubes of many sizes, and presently said: "I'm so glad to have a chance to thank you."

"To thank me—?" He had to wonder.

"I liked your book so much. I think it splendid."

She sat there smiling at him, and he never asked himself which book she meant; for after all he had written three or four. That seemed a vulgar detail, and he wasn't even gratified by the idea of the pleasure she told him—her handsome bright face told him—he had given her. The feeling she appealed to, or at any rate the feeling she excited, was something larger, something that had little to do with any quickened pulsation of his own vanity. It was responsive admiration of the life she embodied, the young purity and richness of which appeared to imply that real success was to resemble *that*, to live, to bloom, to present the perfection of a fine type, not to have hammered out headachy fancies with a bent back at an ink-stained table. While her grey eyes rested on him—there was a wideish space between these, and the division of her rich-coloured hair, so thick that it ventured to be smooth, made a free arch above them—he was almost ashamed of that exercise of the pen which it was her present inclination to commend. He was conscious he should have liked better to please her in some other way. The lines of her face were those of a woman grown, but the child lingered on in her complexion and in the sweetness of her mouth. Above all she was natural—that was indubitable now; more natural than he had supposed at first, perhaps on account of her æsthetic toggery, which was conventionally unconventional, suggesting what he might have called a tortuous spontaneity. He had feared that sort of thing in other cases, and his fears had been justified; for, though he was an artist to the essence, the modern reactionary nymph, with the brambles of the woodland caught in her folds and a look as if the satyrs had toyed with her hair, made him shrink not as a man of starch and patent leather, but as a man potentially himself a poet or even a faun. The girl was really more candid than her costume, and the best proof of it was her supposing her liberal character suited by any uniform. This was a fallacy, since if she was draped as a pessimist he was sure she liked the taste of life. He thanked her for her appreciation—aware at the same time that he didn't appear to thank her enough and that she might think him ungracious. He was afraid she would ask him to explain something he had written, and he always winced at that—perhaps too timidly—for to his own ear the explanation of a work of art sounded fatuous. But he liked her so much as to feel a confidence that in the long run he should be able to show her he wasn't rudely evasive. Moreover she surely wasn't quick to take offence, wasn't irritable; she could be trusted to wait. So when he said to her "Ah don't talk of anything I've done, don't talk of it *here;* there's another man in the house who's the actuality!"—when he uttered this short sincere protest it was with the sense that she would see in the words neither mock humility nor the impatience of a successful man bored with praise.

"You mean Mr. St. George—isn't he delightful?"

Paul Overt met her eyes, which had a cool morning-light that would have half-broken his heart if he hadn't been so young. "Alas I don't know him. I only admire him at a distance."

"Oh you *must* know him—he wants so to talk to you," returned Miss Fancourt, who evidently had the habit of saying the things that, by her quick calculation, would give people pleasure. Paul saw how she would always calculate on everything's being simple between others.

"I shouldn't have supposed he knew anything about me," he professed.

"He does then—everything. And if he didn't I should be able to tell him."

"To tell him everything?" our friend smiled.

"You talk just like the people in your book," she answered.

"Then they must all talk alike."

She thought a moment, not a bit disconcerted. "Well, it must be so difficult. Mr. St. George tells me it *is*—terribly. I've tried too—and I find it so. I've tried to write a novel."

"Mr. St. George oughtn't to discourage you," Paul went so far as to say.

"You do much more—when you wear that expression."

"Well, after all, why try to be an artist?" the young man pursued. "It's so poor—so poor!"

"I don't know what you mean," said Miss Fancourt, who looked grave.

"I mean as compared with being a person of action—as living your works."

"But what's art but an intense life—if it be real?" she asked. "I think it's the only one—everything else is so clumsy!" Her companion laughed, and she brought out with her charming serenity what next struck her. "It's so interesting to meet so many celebrated people."

"So I should think—but surely it isn't new to you."

"Why I've never seen any one—any one: living always in Asia."

The way she talked of Asia somehow enchanted him. "But doesn't that continent swarm with great figures? Haven't you administered provinces in India and had captive rajahs and tributary princes chained to your car?"

It was as if she didn't care even *should* he amuse himself at her cost. "I was with my father, after I left school to go out there. It was delightful being with him—we're alone together in the world, he and I—but there was none of the society I like best. One never heard of a picture— never of a book, except bad ones."

"Never of a picture? Why, wasn't all life a picture?"

She looked over the delightful place where they sat. "Nothing to compare to this. I adore England!" she cried.

It fairly stirred in him the sacred chord. "Ah of course I don't deny that we must do something with her, poor old dear, yet!"

"She hasn't been touched, really," said the girl.

"Did Mr. St. George say that?"

There was a small and, as he felt, harmless spark of irony in his question; which, however, she answered very simply, not noticing the insinuation. "Yes, he says England hasn't been touched—not considering all there is," she went on eagerly. "He's so interesting about our country. To listen to him makes one want so to do something."

"It would make *me* want to," said Paul Overt, feeling strongly, on the instant, the suggestion of what she said and that of the emotion with which she said it, and well aware of what an incentive, on St. George's lips, such a speech might be.

"Oh you—as if you hadn't! I should like so to hear you talk together," she added ardently.

"That's very genial of you; but he'd have it all his own way. I'm prostrate before him."

She had an air of earnestness. "Do you think then he's so perfect?"

"Far from it. Some of his later books seem to me of a queerness—!"

"Yes, yes—he knows that."

Paul Overt stared. "That they seem to me of a queerness—?"

"Well yes, or at any rate that they're not what they should be. He told me he didn't esteem them. He has told me such wonderful things—he's so interesting."

There was a certain shock for Paul Overt in the knowledge that the fine genius they were talking of had been reduced to so explicit a confession and had made it, in his misery, to the first comer; for though Miss Fancourt was charming what was she after all but an immature girl encountered at a country-house? Yet precisely this was part of the sentiment he himself had just expressed: he would make way completely for the poor peccable great man not because he didn't read him clear, but altogether because he did. His consideration was half composed of tenderness for superficialities which he was sure their perpetrator judged privately, judged more ferociously than any one, and which represented some tragic intellectual secret. He would have his reasons for his psychology *à fleur de peau,* and these reasons could only be cruel ones, such as would make him dearer to those who already were fond of him. "You excite my envy. I have my reserves, I discriminate—but I love him," Paul said in a moment. "And seeing him for the first time this way is a great event for me."

"How momentous—how magnificent!" cried the girl. "How delicious to bring you together!"

"*Your* doing it—that makes it perfect," our friend returned.

"He's as eager as you," she went on. "But it's so odd you shouldn't have met."

"It's not really so odd as it strikes you. I've been out of England so much—made repeated absences all these last years."

She took this in with interest. "And yet you write of it as well as if you were always here."

"It's just the being away perhaps. At any rate the best bits, I suspect, are those that were done in dreary places abroad."

"And why were they dreary?"

"Because they were health-resorts—where my poor mother was dying."

"Your poor mother?"—she was all sweet wonder.

"We went from place to place to help her to get better. But she never did. To the deadly Riviera, (I hate it!) to the high Alps, to Algiers, and far away—a hideous journey —to Colorado."

"And she isn't better?" Miss Fancourt went on.

"She died a year ago."

"Really?—like mine! Only that's years since. Some day you must tell me about your mother," she added.

He could at first, on this, only gaze at her. "What right things you say! If you say them to St. George I don't wonder he's in bondage."

It pulled her up for a moment. "I don't know what you mean. He doesn't make speeches and professions at all— he isn't ridiculous."

"I'm afraid you consider then that I am."

"No, I don't"—she spoke it rather shortly. And then she added: "He understands—understands everything."

The young man was on the point of saying jocosely: "And I don't—is that it?" But these words, in time, changed themselves to others slightly less trivial. "Do you suppose he understands his wife?"

Miss Fancourt made no direct answer, but after a moment's hesitation put it: "Isn't she charming?"

"Not in the least!"

"Here he comes. Now you must know him," she went on. A small group of visitors had gathered at the other end of the gallery and had been there overtaken by Henry St. George, who strolled in from a neighbouring room. He stood near them a moment, not falling into the talk but taking up an old miniature from a table and vaguely regarding it. At the end of a minute he became aware of Miss Fancourt and her companion in the distance; whereupon, laying down his miniature, he approached them with the same procrastinating air, his hands in his pockets and his eyes turned, right and left, to the pictures. The gallery was so long that this transit took some little time, especially as there was a moment when he stopped to admire the fine Gainsborough. "He says Mrs. St. George has been the making of him," the girl continued in a voice slightly lowered.

"Ah he's often obscure!" Paul laughed.

"Obscure?" she repeated as if she heard it for the first time. Her eyes rested on her other friend, and it wasn't lost upon Paul that they appeared to send out great shafts of softness. "He's going to speak to us!" she fondly breathed. There was a sort of rapture in her voice, and our friend was startled. "Bless my soul, does she care for him like *that?*—is she in love with him?" he mentally enquired. "Didn't I tell you he was eager?" she had meanwhile asked of him.

"It's eagerness dissimulated," the young man returned as the subject of their observation lingered before his Gainsborough. "He edges toward us shyly. Does he mean that she saved him by burning that book?"

"That book? what book did she burn?" The girl quickly turned her face to him.

"Hasn't he told you then?"

"Not a word."

"Then he doesn't tell you everything!" Paul had guessed that she pretty much supposed he did. The great man had now resumed his course and come nearer; in spite of which his more qualified admirer risked a profane observation. "St. George and the Dragon is what the anecdote suggests!"

His companion, however, didn't hear it; she smiled at the dragon's adversary. "He *is* eager—he is!" she insisted.

"Eager for you—yes."

But meanwhile she had called out: "I'm sure you want to know Mr. Overt. You'll be great friends, and it will always be delightful to me to remember I was here when you first met and that I had something to do with it."

There was a freshness of intention in the words that carried them off; nevertheless our young man was sorry for Henry St. George, as he was sorry at any time for any person publicly invited to be responsive and delightful. He would have been so touched to believe that a man he deeply admired should care a straw for him that he wouldn't play with such a presumption if it were possibly vain. In a single glance of the eye of the pardonable master he read—having the sort of divination that belonged to his talent—that his personage had ever a store of friendly patience, which was part of his rich outfit, but was versed in no printed page of a rising scribbler. There was even a relief, a simplification, in that: liking him so much already for what he had done, how could one have liked him any more for a perception which must at the best have been vague? Paul Overt got up, trying to show his compassion, but at the same instant he found himself encompassed by St. George's happy personal art— a manner of which it was the essence to conjure away false positions. It all took place in a moment. Paul was conscious that he knew him now, conscious of his handshake and of the very quality of his hand; of his face, seen nearer and consequently seen better, of a general fraternising assurance, and in particular of the circumstance that St. George didn't dislike him (as yet at least) for being imposed by a charming but too gushing girl, attractive enough without such danglers. No irritation at any rate was reflected in the voice with which he questioned Miss Fancourt as to some project of a walk—a general walk of the company round the park. He had soon said something to Paul about a talk—"We must have a tremendous lot of talk; there are so many things, aren't there?"—but our friend could see this idea wouldn't in the present case take very immediate effect. All the same he was extremely happy, even after the matter of the walk had been settled—the three presently passed back to the other part of the gallery, where it was discussed with several members of the party; even when, after they had all gone out together, he found himself for half an hour conjoined with Mrs. St. George. Her husband had taken the advance with Miss Fancourt, and this pair were quite out of sight. It was the prettiest of rambles for a summer afternoon—a grassy circuit, of immense extent, skirting the limit of the park within. The park was completely surrounded by its old mottled but perfect red wall, which, all the way on their left, constituted in itself an object of interest. Mrs. St. George mentioned to him the surprising number of acres thus enclosed, together with numerous other facts relating to the property and the family, and the family's other properties: she couldn't too strongly urge on him the importance of seeing their other houses. She ran over the names of these and rang the changes on them with the facility of practice, making them appear an almost endless list. She had received Paul Overt very amiably on his breaking ground with her by the mention of his joy in having just made her husband's acquaintance, and struck him as so alert and so accomodating a little woman that he was rather ashamed of his *mot* about her to Miss Fancourt; though he reflected that a hundred other people, on a hundred occasions, would have been sure to make it. He got on with Mrs. St.

George, in short, better than he expected; but this didn't prevent her suddenly becoming aware that she was faint with fatigue and must take her way back to the house by the shortest cut. She professed that she hadn't the strength of a kitten and was a miserable wreck; a character he had been too preoccupied to discern in her while he wondered in what sense she could be held to have been the making of her husband. He had arrived at a glimmering of the answer when she announced that she must leave him, though this perception was of course provisional. While he was in the very act of placing himself at her disposal for the return the situation underwent a change; Lord Masham had suddenly turned up, coming back to them, overtaking them, emerging from the shrubbery—Overt could scarcely have said how he appeared—and Mrs. St. George had protested that she wanted to be left alone and not to break up the party. A moment later she was walking off with Lord Masham. Our friend fell back and joined Lady Watermouth, to whom he presently mentioned that Mrs. St. George had been obliged to renounce the attempt to go further.

"She oughtn't to have come out at all," her ladyship rather grumpily remarked.

"Is she so very much of an invalid?"

"Very bad indeed." And his hostess added with still greater austerity: "She oughtn't really to come to one!" He wondered what was implied by this, and presently gathered that it was not a reflexion on the lady's conduct or her moral nature: it only represented that her strength was not equal to her aspirations.

III

THE smoking-room at Summersoft was on the scale of the rest of the place—high, light, commodious and decorated with such refined old carvings and mouldings that it seemed rather a bower for ladies who should sit at work at fading crewels than a parliament of gentlemen smoking strong cigars. The gentlemen mustered there in considerable force on the Sunday evening, collecting mainly at one end, in front of one of the cool fair fireplaces of white marble, the entablature of which was adorned with a delicate little Italian "subject." There was another in the wall that faced it, and, thanks to the mild summer night, a fire in neither; but a nucleus for aggregation was furnished on one side by table in the chimney-corner laden with bottles, decanters and tall tumblers. Paul Overt was a faithless smoker; he would puff a cigarette for reasons with which tobacco had nothing to do. This was particularly the case on the occasion of which I speak; his motive was the vision of a little direct talk with Henry St. George. The "tremendous" communion of which the great man had held out hopes to him earlier in the day had not yet come off, and this saddened him considerably, for the party was to go its several ways immediately after breakfast on the morrow. He had, however, the disappointment of finding that apparently the author of "shadowmere" was not disposed to prolong his vigil. He wasn't among the gentlemen assembled when Paul entered, nor was he one of those who turned up, in bright habiliments, during the next ten minutes. The young man waited a little, wondering if he had only gone to put on something extraordinary; this would account for his delay as well as contribute further to Overt's impression of his tendency to do the approved superficial thing. But he didn't arrive—he must have been putting on something more extraordinary than was probable. Our hero gave him up, feeling a little injured, a little wounded, at this loss of twenty coveted words. He wasn't angry, but he puffed his cigarette sighingly, with the sense of something rare possibly missed. He wandered away with his regret and moved slowly round the room, looking at the old prints on the walls. In this attitude he presently felt a hand on his shoulder and a friendly voice in his ear "This is good. I hoped I should find you. I came down on purpose." St. George was there without a change of dress and with a fine face—his graver one—to which our young man all in a flutter responded. He explained that it was only for the Master—the idea of a little talk—that he had sat up, and that, not finding him, he had been on the point of going to bed.

"Well, you know, I don't smoke—my wife doesn't let me," said St. George, looking for a place to sit down. "It's very good for me—very good for me. Let us take that sofa."

"Do you mean smoking's good for you?"

"No, no—her not letting me. It's a great thing to have a wife who's so sure of all the things one can do without. One might never find them out one's self. She doesn't allow me to touch a cigarette." They took possession of a sofa at a distance from the group of smokers, and St. George went on: "Have you got one yourself?"

"Do you mean a cigarette?"

"Dear no—a wife!"

"No; and yet I'd give up my cigarette for one."

"You'd give up a good deal more than that," St. George returned. "However, you'd get a great deal in return. There's a something to be said for wives," he added, folding his arms and crossing his outstretched legs. He declined tobacco altogether and sat there without returning fire. His companion stopped smoking, touched by his courtesy; and after all they were out of the fumes, their sofa was in

a far-away corner. It would have been a mistake, St.
George went on, a great mistake for them to have separated
without a little chat; "for I know all about you," he said,
"I know you're very remarkable. You've written a very
distinguished book."

"And how do you know it?" Paul asked.

"Why, my dear fellow, it's in the air, it's in the papers,
it's everywhere." St. George spoke with the immediate
familiarity of a confrère—a tone that seemed to his neigh-
bour the very rustle of the laurel. "You're on all men's lips
and, what's better, on all women's. And I've just been reading your book."

"Just? You hadn't read it this afternoon," said Overt.

"How do you know that?"

"I think you should know how I know it," the young
man laughed.

"I suppose Miss Fancourt told you."

"No indeed—she led me rather to suppose you had."

"Yes—that's much more what she'd do. Doesn't she shed
a rosy glow over life? But you didn't believe her?" asked
St. George.

"No, not when you came to us there."

"Did I pretend? did I pretend badly?" But without
waiting for an answer to this St. George went on: "You
ought always to believe such a girl as that—always,
always. Some women are meant to be taken with allowances and reserves; but you must take *her* just as she is."

"I like her very much," said Paul Overt.

Something in his tone appeared to excite on his companion's part a momentary sense of the absurd; perhaps
it was the air of deliberation attending this judgment.
St. George broke into a laugh to reply. "It's the best thing
you can do with her. She's a rare young lady! In point of
fact, however, I confess I hadn't read you this afternoon."

"Then you see how right I was in this particular case
not to believe Miss Fancourt."

"How right? how can I agree to that when I lost credit by it?"

"Do you wish to pass exactly for what she represents you? Certainly you needn't be afraid," Paul said.

"Ah, my dear young man, don't talk about passing— for the likes of me! I'm passing away—nothing else than that. She has a better use for her young imagination (isn't it fine?) than in 'representing' in any way such a weary wasted used-up animal!" The Master spoke with a sudden sadness that produced a protest on Paul's part; but before the protest could be uttered he went on, reverting to the latter's striking novel: "I had no idea you were so good— one hears of so many things. But you're surprisingly good."

"I'm going to be surprisingly better," Overt made bold to reply.

"I see that, and it's what fetches me. I don't see so much else—as one looks about—that's going to be surprisingly better. They're going to be consistently worse—most of the things. It's so much easier to be worse—heaven knows I've found it so. I'm not in a great glow, you know, about what's breaking out all over the place. But you *must* be better, you really must keep it up. I haven't of course. It's very difficult—that's the devil of the whole thing, keeping it up. But I see you'll be able to. It will be a great disgrace if you don't."

"It's very interesting to hear you speak of yourself; but I don't know what you mean by your allusions to your having fallen off," Paul Overt observed with pardonable hypocrisy. He liked his companion so much now that the fact of any decline of talent or of care had ceased for the moment to be vivid to him.

"Don't say that—don't say that," St. George returned gravely, his head resting on the top of the sofa-back and his eyes on the ceiling. "You know perfectly what I mean. I haven't read twenty pages of your book without seeing that you can't help it."

"You make me very miserable," Paul ecstatically breathed.

"I'm glad of that, for it may serve as a kind of warning. Shocking enough it must be, especially to a young fresh mind, full of faith—the spectacle of a man meant for better things sunk at my age in such dishonour." St. George, in the same contemplative attitude, spoke softly but deliberately, and without perceptible emotion. His tone indeed suggested an impersonal lucidity that was practically cruel —cruel to himself—and made his young friend lay an argumentative hand on his arm. But he went on while his eyes seemed to follow the graces of the eighteenth-century ceiling: "Look at me well, take my lesson to heart—for it *is* a lesson. Let that good come of it at least that you shudder with your pitiful impression, and that this may help to keep you straight in the future. Don't become in your old age what I have in mine—the depressing, the deplorable illustration of the worship of false gods!"

"What do you mean by your old age?" the young man asked.

"It has made me old. But I like your youth."

Paul answered nothing—they sat for a minute in silence. They heard the others going on about the governmental majority. Then "What do you mean by false gods?" he enquired.

His companion had no difficulty whatever in saying, "The idols of the market; money and luxury and 'the world'; placing one's children and dressing one's wife; everything that drives one to the short and easy way. Ah, the vile things they make one do!"

"But surely one's right to want to place one's children."

"One has no business to have any children," St. George placidly declared. "I mean of course if one wants to do anything good."

"But aren't they an inspiration—an incentive?"

"An incentive to damnation, artistically speaking."

"You touch on very deep things—things I should like

to discuss with you," Paul said. "I should like you to tell me volumes about yourself. This is a great feast for *me!*"

"Of course it is, cruel youth. But to show you I'm still not incapable, degraded as I am, of an act of faith, I'll tie my vanity to the stake for you and burn it to ashes. You must come and see me—you must come and see us," the Master quickly substituted. "Mrs. St. George is charming; I don't know whether you've had any opportunity to talk with her. She'll be delighted to see you; she likes great celebrities, whether incipient or predominant. You must come and dine—my wife will write to you. Where are you to be found?"

"This is my little address"—and Overt drew out his pocketbook and extracted a visiting-card. On second thoughts, however, he kept it back, remarking that he wouldn't trouble his friend to take charge of it but would come and see him straightway in London and leave it at his door if he should fail to obtain entrance.

"Ah you'll probably fail; my wife's always out—or when she isn't out is knocked up from having *been* out. You must come and dine—though that won't do much good either, for my wife insists on big dinners." St. George turned it over further, but then went on: "You must come down and see us in the country, that's the best way; we've plenty of room and it isn't bad."

"You've a house in the country?" Paul asked enviously.

"Ah not like this! But we have a sort of place we go to—an hour from Euston. That's one of the reasons."

"One of the reasons?"

"Why my books are so bad."

"You must tell me all the others!" Paul longingly laughed.

His friend made no direct rejoinder to this, but spoke again abruptly. "Why have I never seen you before?"

The tone of the question was singularly flattering to our hero, who felt it to imply the great man's now perceiving he had for years missed something. "Partly, I suppose, because there has been no particular reason why you should see me. I haven't lived in the world—in your world. I've spent many years out of England, in different places abroad."

"Well, please don't do it any more. You must do Eng-land—there's such a lot of it."

"Do you mean I must write about it?"—and Paul struck the note of the listening candour of a child.

"Of course you must. And tremendously well, do you mind? That takes off a little of my esteem for this thing of yours—that it goes on abroad. Hang 'abroad'! Stay at home and do things here—do subjects we can measure."

"I'll do whatever you tell me," Overt said, deeply at-tentive. "But pardon me if I say I don't understand how you've been reading my book," he added. "I've had you before me all the afternoon, first in that long walk, then at tea on the lawn, till we went to dress for dinner, and all the evening at dinner and in this place."

St. George turned his face about with a smile. "I gave it but a quarter of an hour."

"A quarter of an hour's immense, but I don't under-stand where you put it in. In the drawing-room after dinner you weren't reading—you were talking to Miss Fancourt."

"It comes to the same thing, because we talked about 'Ginistrella.' She described it to me—she lent me her copy."

"Lent it to you?"

"She travels with it."

"It's incredible," Paul blushed.

"It's glorious for you, but it also turned out very well for me. When the ladies went off to bed she kindly offered to send the book down to me. Her maid brought it to me in the hall, and I went to my room with it. I hadn't thought of coming here, I do that so little. But I don't sleep early, I always have to read an hour or two. I sat down to your novel on the spot, without undressing, without taking off anything but my coat. I think that's a sign my curiosity had been strongly roused about it. I read a quarter of an hour, as I tell you, and even in a quarter of an hour I was greatly struck."

"Ah the beginning isn't very good—it's—the whole thing!" said Overt, who had listened to this recital with extreme interest. "And you laid down the book and came after me?" he asked.

"That's the way it moved me. I said to myself 'I see it's off his own bat, and he's there, by the way, and the day's over, and I haven't said twenty words to him.' It occurred to me that you'd probably be in the smoking-room and that it wouldn't be too late to repair my omission. I wanted to do something civil to you, so I put on my coat and came down. I shall read your book again when I go up."

Our friend faced round in his place—he was touched as he had scarce ever been by the picture of such a demonstration in his favour. "You're really the kindest of men. Cela s'est passé comme ça?—and I've been sitting here with you all this time and never apprehended it and never thanked you!"

"Thank Miss Fancourt—it was she who wound me up. She has made me feel as if I had read your novel."

"She's an angel from heaven!" Paul declared.

"She is indeed. I've never seen any one like her. Her interest in literature's touching—something quite peculiar to herself; she takes it all so seriously. She feels the arts and she wants to feel them more. To those who practise them it's almost humiliating—her curiosity, her sympathy, her good faith. How can anything be as fine as she supposes it?"

"She's a rare organisation," the younger man sighed.

"The richest I've ever seen—an artistic intelligence really of the first order. And lodged in such a form!" St. George exclaimed.

"One would like to represent such a girl as that," Paul continued.

"Ah there it is—there's nothing like life!" said his companion. "When you're finished, squeezed dry and used up and you think the sack's empty, you're still appealed to, you still get touches and thrills, the idea springs up—out of the lap of the actual—and shows you there's always something to be done. But I shan't do it—she's not for me!"

"How do you mean, not for you?"

"Oh it's all over—she's for you, if you like."

"Ah much less!" said Paul. "She's not for a dingy little man of letters; she's for the world, the bright rich world of bribes and rewards. And the world will take hold of her—it will carry her away."

"It will try—but it's just a case in which there may be a fight. It would be worth fighting, for a man who had it in him, with youth and talent on his side."

These words rang not a little in Paul Overt's consciousness—they held him briefly silent. "It's a wonder she has remained as she is; giving herself away so—with so much to give away."

"Remaining, you mean, so ingenuous —so natural? Oh she doesn't care a straw—she gives away because she overflows. She has her own feelings, her own standards; she doesn't keep remembering that she must be proud. And then she hasn't been here long enough to be spoiled; she has picked up a fashion or two, but only the amusing ones. She's a provincial—a provincial of genius," St. George went on; "her very blunders are charming, her mistakes are interesting. She has come back from Asia with all sorts of excited curiosities and unappeased appetites. She's first-rate herself and she expends herself on the second-rate. She's life herself and she takes a rare interest in imitations. She mixes all things up, but there are none in regard to which she hasn't perceptions. She sees things in a perspective—as if from the top of the Himalayas—and she enlarges everything she touches. Above all she exaggerates—to herself. I mean. She exaggerates you and me!"

There was nothing in that description to allay the agi-

tation caused in our younger friend by such a sketch of
a fine subject. It seemed to him to show the art of St.
George's admired hand, and he lost himself in gazing at
the vision—this hovered there before him—of a woman's
figure which should be part of the glory of a novel. But at
the end of a moment the thing had turned into smoke,
and out of the smoke—the last puff of a big cigar—proceeded the voice of General Fancourt, who had left the
others and come and planted himself before the gentlemen
on the sofa. "I suppose that when you fellows get talking
you sit up half the night."

"Half the night?—jamais de la vie! I follow a hygiene"
—and St. George rose to his feet.

"I see—you're hothouse plants," laughed the General.
"That's the way you produce your flowers."

"I produce mine between ten and one every morning—
I bloom with a regularity!" St. George went on.

"And with a splendour!" added the polite General, while
Paul noted how little the author of "Shadowmere" minded,
as he phrased it to himself, when addressed as a celebrated
story-teller. The young man had an idea *he* should never
get used to that; it would always make him uncomfortable
—from the suspicion that people would think they had
to—and he would want to prevent it. Evidently his great
colleague had toughened and hardened—had made himself
a surface. The group of men had finished their cigars and
taken up their bedroom candlesticks; but before they all
passed out Lord Watermouth invited the pair of guests
who had been so absorbed together to "have" something.
It happened that they both declined; upon which General
Fancourt said: "Is that the hygiene? You don't water the
flowers?"

"Oh I should drown them!" St. George replied; but,
leaving the room still at his young friend's sides, he added
whimsically, for the latter's benefit, in a lower tone: "My
wife doesn't let me."

"Well I'm glad I'm not one of you fellows!" the General richly concluded.

The nearness of Summersoft to London had this consequence, chilling to a person who had had a vision of sociability in a railway-carriage, that most of the company, after breakfast, drove back to town, entering their own vehicles, which had come out to fetch them, while their servants returned by train with their luggage. Three or four young men, among whom was Paul Overt, also availed themselves of the common convenience; but they stood in the portico of the house and saw the others roll away. Miss Fancourt got into a victoria with her father after she had shaken hands with our hero and said, smiling in the frankest way in the world, "I *must* see you more. Mrs. St. George is so nice; she has promised to ask us both to dinner together." This lady and her husband took their places in a perfectly-appointed brougham—she required a closed carriage—and as our young man waved his hat to them in response to their nods and flourishes he reflected that, taken together, they were an honourable image of success, of the material rewards and the social credit of literature. Such things were not the full measure, but he nevertheless felt a little proud for literature.

IV

BEFORE a week had elapsed he met Miss Fancourt in
Bond Street, at a private view of the works of a young
artist in "black-and-white" who had been so good as to
invite him to the stuffy scene. The drawings were admirable, but the crowd in the one little room was so dense
that he felt himself up to his neck in a sack of wool. A
fringe of people at the outer edge endeavoured by curving
forward their backs and presenting, below them, a still
more convex surface of resistance to the pressure of the
mass, to preserve an interval between their noses and the
glazed mounts of the pictures; while the central body,
in the comparative gloom projected by a wide horizontal
screen hung under the skylight and allowing only a margin
for the day, remained upright dense and vague, lost in the
contemplation of its own ingredients. This contemplation
sat especially in the sad eyes of certain female heads, sur-
mounted with hats of strange convolution and plumage,
which rose on long necks above the others. One of the
heads, Paul perceived, was much the most beautiful of the
collection, and his next discovery was that it belonged to
Miss Fancourt. Its beauty was enhanced by the glad smile
she sent him across surrounding obstructions, a smile that
drew him to her as fast as he could make his way. He had
seen for himself at Summersoft that the last thing her
nature contained was an affectation of indifference; yet
even with this circumspection he took a fresh satisfaction
in her not having pretended to await his arrival with composure. She smiled as radiantly as if she wished to make
him hurry, and as soon as he came within earshot she broke
out in her voice of joy: "He's here—he's here; he's coming
back in a moment!"

"Ah your father?" Paul returned as she offered him her hand.

"Oh dear no, this isn't in my poor father's line. I mean Mr. St. George. He has just left me to speak to some one— he's coming back. It's he who brought me—wasn't it charming?"

"Ah that gives him a pull over me—I couldn't have 'brought' you, could I?"

"If you had been so kind as to propose it—why not you as well as he?" the girl returned with a face that, expressing no cheap coquetry, simply affirmed a happy fact.

"Why he's a *père de famille*. They've privileges," Paul explained. And then quickly: "Will you go to see places with *me?*" he asked.

"Anything you like," she smiled. "I know what you mean, that girls have to have a lot of people—!" Then she broke off: "I don't know; I'm free. I've always been like that—I can go about with any one. I'm so glad to meet you," she added with a sweet distinctness that made those near her turn round.

"Let me at least repay that speech by taking you out of this squash," her friend said. "Surely people aren't happy here!"

"No, they're awfully *mornes*, aren't they? But I'm very happy indeed and I promised Mr. St. George to remain on this spot till he comes back. He's going to take me away. They send him invitations for things of this sort—more than he wants. It was so kind of him to think of me."

"They also send me invitations of this kind—more than I want. And if thinking of *you* will do it—!" Paul went on.

"Oh I delight in them—everything that's life, everything that's London!"

"They don't have private views in Asia, I suppose," he laughed. "But what a pity that for this year, even in this gorged city, they're pretty well over."

"Well, next year will do, for I hope you believe we're

going to be friends always. Here he comes!" Miss Fan-court continued before Paul had time to respond.

He made out St. George in the gaps of the crowd, and this perhaps led to his hurrying a little to say: "I hope that doesn't mean I'm to wait till next year to see you."

"No, no—aren't we to meet at dinner on the twenty-fifth?" she panted with an eagerness as happy as his own.

"That's almost next year. Is there no means of seeing you before?"

She stared with all her brightness. "Do you mean you'd come?"

"Like a shot, if you'll be so good as to ask me!"

"On Sunday then—this next Sunday?"

"What have I done that you should doubt it?" the young man asked with delight.

Miss Fancourt turned instantly to St. George, who had now joined them, and announced triumphantly: "He's coming on Sunday—this next Sunday!"

"Ah my day—my day too!" said the famous novelist, laughing, to their companion.

"Yes, but not yours only. You shall meet in Manchester Square; you shall talk—you shall be wonderful!"

"We don't meet often enough," St. George allowed shaking hands with his disciple. "Too many things—ah too many things! But we must make it up in the country in September. You won't forget you've promised me that?"

"Why he's coming on the twenty-fifth—you'll see him then," said the girl.

"On the twenty-fifth?" St. George asked vaguely.

"We dine with you; I hope you haven't forgotten. He's dining out that day," she added gaily to Paul.

"Oh bless me, yes—that's charming! And you're com-ing? My wife didn't tell me," St. George said to him. "Too many things—too many things!" he repeated.

"Too many people—too many people!" Paul exclaimed, giving ground before the penetration of an elbow.

"You oughtn't to say that. They all read you."

"Me? I should like to see them! Only two or three at most," the young man returned.

"Did you ever hear anything like that? He knows, haughtily, how good he is!" St. George declared, laughing, to Miss Fancourt. "They read *me,* but that doesn't make me like them any better. Come away from them, come away!" And he led the way out of the exhibition.

"He's going to take me to the Park," Miss Fancourt observed to Overt with elation as they passed along the corridor that led to the street.

"Ah does he go there?" Paul asked, taking the fact for a somewhat unexpected illustration of St. George's *mœurs.*

"It's a beautiful day—there'll be a great crowd. We're going to look at the people, to look at types," the girl went on. "We shall sit under the trees; we shall walk by the Row."

"I go once a year—on business," said St. George, who had overheard Paul's question.

"Or with a country cousin, didn't you tell me? I'm the country cousin!" she continued over her shoulder to Paul as their friend drew her toward a hansom to which he had signalled. The young man watched them get in; he returned, as he stood there, the friendly wave of the hand with which, ensconced in the vehicle beside her, St. George took leave of him. He even lingered to see the vehicle start away and lose itself in the confusion of Bond Street. He followed it with his eyes; it put to him embarrassing things. "She's not for *me!*" the great novelist had said emphatically at Summersoft; but his manner of conducting himself toward her appeared not quite in harmony with such a conviction. How could he have behaved differently if she *had* been for him? An indefinite envy rose in Paul Overt's heart as he took his way on foot alone; a feeling addressed alike, strangely enough, to each of the occupants of the hansom. How much he should like to rattle about London with such a girl! How much he should like to go and look at "types" with St. George!

The next Sunday at four o'clock he called in Manchester Square, where his secret wish was gratified by his finding Miss Fancourt alone. She was in a large bright friendly occupied room, which was painted red all over, draped with the quaint cheap florid stuffs that are represented as coming from southern and eastern countries, where they are fabled to serve as the counterpanes of the peasantry, and bedecked with pottery of vivid hues, ranged on casual shelves, and with many water-colour drawings from the hand (as the visitor learned) of the young lady herself, commemorating with a brave breadth the sunsets, the mountains, the temples and palaces of India. He sat an hour—more than an hour, two hours— and all the while no one came in. His hostess was so good as to remark, with her liberal humanity, that it was delightful they weren't interrupted: it was so rare in London, especially at that season, that people got a good talk. But luckily now, of a fine Sunday, half the world went out of town, and that made it better for those who didn't go, when these others were in sympathy. It was the defect of London—one of two or three, the very short list of those she recognised in the teeming world-city she adored —that there were too few good chances for talk: you never had time to carry anything far.

"Too many things, too many things!" Paul said, quoting St. George's exclamation of a few days before.

"Ah yes, for him there are too many—his life's too complicated."

"Have you seen it *near*? That's what I should like to do; it might explain some mysteries," her visitor went on. She asked him what mysteries he meant, and he said: "Oh peculiarities of his work, inequalities, superficialities. For one who looks at it from the artistic point of view it contains a bottomless ambiguity."

She became at this, on the spot, all intensity. "Ah do

describe that more—it's so interesting. There are no such suggestive questions. I'm so fond of them. He thinks he's a failure—fancy!" she beautifully wailed.

"That depends on what his ideal may have been. With his gifts it ought to have been high. But till one knows what he really proposed to himself—! Do *you* know by chance?" the young man broke off.

"Oh he doesn't talk to me about himself. I can't make him. It's too provoking."

Paul was on the point of asking what then he did talk about, but discretion checked it and he said instead: "Do you think he's unhappy at home?"

She seemed to wonder. "At home?"

"I mean in his relations with his wife. He has a mystifying little way of alluding to her."

"Not to me," said Marian Fancourt with her clear eyes. "That wouldn't be right, would it?" she asked gravely.

"Not particularly; so I'm glad he doesn't mention her to you. To praise her might bore you, and he has no business to do anything else. Yet he knows you better than me."

"Ah but he respects *you!*" the girl cried as with envy.

Her visitor stared a moment, then broke into a laugh. "Doesn't he respect you?"

"Of course, but not in the same way. He respects what you've done—he told me so the other day."

Paul drank it in, but retained his faculties. "When you went to look at types?"

"Yes—we found so many: he has such an observation of them! He talked a great deal about your book. He says it's really important."

"Important! Ah the grand creature!"—and the author of the work in question groaned for joy.

"He was wonderfully amusing, he was inexpressibly droll, while we walked about. He sees everything; he has so many comparisons and images, and they're always exactly right. C'est d'un trouvé, as they say!"

"Yes, with his gifts, such things as he ought to have done!" Paul sighed.

"And don't you think he *has* done them?"

Ah it was just the point. "A part of them, and of course even that part's immense. But he might have been one of the greatest. However, let us not make this an hour of qualifications. Even as they stand," our friend earnestly concluded, "his writings are a mine of gold."

To this proposition she ardently responded, and for half an hour the pair talked over the Master's principal productions. She knew them well—she knew them even better than her visitor, who was struck with her critical intelligence and with something large and bold in the movement in her mind. She said things that startled him and that evidently had come to her directly; they weren't picked-up phrases—she placed them too well. St. George had been right about her being first-rate, about her not being afraid to gush, not remembering that she must be proud. Suddenly something came back to her, and she said: "I recollect that he did speak of Mrs. St. George to me once. He said, apropos of something or other, that she didn't care for perfection."

"That's a great crime in an artist's wife," Paul returned.

"Yes, poor thing!" and the girl sighed with a suggestion of many reflexions, some of them mitigating. But she presently added: "Ah perfection, perfection—how one ought to go in for it! I wish *I* could."

"Every one can in his way," her companion opined.

"In *his* way, yes—but not in hers. Women are so hampered—so condemned! Yet it's a kind of dishonour if you don't, when you want to *do* something, isn't it?" Miss Fancourt pursued, dropping one train in her quickness to take up another, an accident that was common with her. So these two young persons sat discussing high themes in their eclectic drawing-room, in their London "season" —discussing, with extreme seriousness, the high theme of perfection. It must be said in extenuation of this eccentricity that they were interested in the business. Their tone had truth and their emotion beauty; they weren't posturing for each other or for some one else.

The subject was so wide that they found themselves reducing it; the perfection to which for the moment they agreed to confine their speculations was that of the valid the exemplary work of art. Our young woman's imagination, it appeared, had wandered far in that direction, and her guest had the rare delight of feeling in their conversation a full interchange. This episode will have lived for years in his memory and even in his wonder; it had the quality that fortune distils in a single drop at a time—the quality that lubricates many ensuing frictions. He still, whenever he likes, has a vision of the room, the bright red sociable talkative room with the curtains that, by a stroke of successful audacity, had the note of vivid blue. He remembers where certain things stood, the particular book open on the table and the almost intense odour of the flowers placed, at the left, somewhere behind him. These facts were the fringe, as it were, of a fine special agitation which had its birth in those two hours and of which perhaps the main sign was in its leading him inwardly and repeatedly to breathe "I had no idea there was any one like this—I had no idea there was any one like this!" Her freedom amazed him and charmed him—it seemed so to simplify the practical question. She was on the footing of an independent personage—a motherless girl who had passed out of her teens and had a position and responsibilities, who wasn't held down to the limitations of a little miss. She came and went with no dragged duenna, she received people alone, and, though she was totally without hardness, the question of protection or patronage had no relevancy in regard to her. She gave such an impression of the clear and the noble combined with the easy and the natural that in spite of her eminent modern situation she suggested no sort of sisterhood with the "fast" girl. Modern she was indeed, and made Paul

Overt, who loved old colour, the golden glaze of time, think with some alarm of the muddled palette of the future. He couldn't get used to her interest in the arts he cared for; it seemed too good to be real—it was so unlikely an adventure to tumble into such a well of sympathy. One might stray into the desert easily—that was on the cards and that was the law of life; but it was too rare an accident to stumble on a crystal well. Yet if her aspirations seemed at one moment too extravagant to be real they struck him at the next as too intelligent to be false. They were both high and lame, and, whims for whims, he preferred them to any he had met in a like relation. It was probable enough she would leave them behind—exchange them for politics or "smartness" or mere prolific maternity, as was the custom of scribbling daubing educated flattered girls in an age of luxury and a society of leisure. He noted that the water-colours on the walls of the room she sat in had mainly the quality of being naïves, and reflected that naïveté in art is like a zero in a number: its importance depends on the figure it is united with. Meanwhile, however, he had fallen in love with her. Before he went away, at any rate, he said to her: "I thought St. George was coming to see you to-day, but he doesn't turn up."

For a moment he supposed she was going to cry "Comment donc? Did you come here only to meet him?" But the next he became aware of how little such a speech would have fallen in with any note of flirtation he had as yet perceived in her. She only replied: "Ah yes, but I don't think he'll come. He recommended me not to expect him." Then she gaily but all gently added: "He said it wasn't fair to you. But I think I could manage two."

"So could I," Paul Overt returned, stretching the point a little to meet her. In reality his appreciation of the occasion was so completely an appreciation of the woman before him that another figure in the scene, even so esteemed a one as St. George, might for the hour have

appealed to him vainly. He left the house wondering
what the great man had meant by its not being fair to
him; and, still more than that, whether he had actually
stayed away from the force of that idea. As he took his
course through the Sunday solitude of Manchester Square,
swinging his stick and with a good deal of emotion fer-
menting in his soul, it appeared to him he was living in a
world strangely magnanimous. Miss Fancourt had told
him it was possible she should be away, and that her
father should be, on the following Sunday, but that she
had the hope of a visit from him in the other event. She
promised to let him know should their absence fail, and
then he might act accordingly. After he had passed into
one of the streets that open from the Square he stopped
without definite intentions, looking sceptically for a cab.
In a moment he saw a hansom roll through the place from
the other side and come a part of the way toward him.
He was on the point of hailing the driver when he noticed
a "fare" within; then he waited, seeing the man prepare
to deposit his passenger by pulling up at one of the houses.
The house was apparently the one he himself had just
quitted; at least he drew that inference as he recognised
Henry St. George in the person who stepped out of the
hansom. Paul turned off as quickly as if he had been caught
in the act of spying. He gave up his cab—he preferred to
walk; he would go nowhere else. He was glad St. George
hadn't renounced his visit altogether—that would have
been too absurd. Yes, the world was magnanimous, and
even he himself felt so as, on looking at his watch, he noted
but six o'clock, so that he could mentally congratulate
his successor on having an hour still to sit in Miss Fancourt's drawing-room. He himself might use that hour for
another visit, but by the time he reached the Marble Arch
the idea of such a course had become incongruous to him.
He passed beneath that architectural effort and walked
into the Park till he had got upon the spreading grass.
Here he continued to walk; he took his way across the

elastic turf and came out by the Serpentine. He watched with a friendly eye the diversions of the London people, he bent a glance almost encouraging on the young ladies paddling their sweethearts about the lake and the guardsmen tickling tenderly with their bearskins the artificial flowers in the Sunday hats of their partners. He prolonged his meditative walk; he went into Kensington Gardens, he sat upon the penny chairs, he looked at the little sailboats launched upon the round pond and was glad he had no engagement to dine. He repaired for this purpose, very late, to his club, where he found himself unable to order a repast and told the waiter to bring whatever there was. He didn't even observe what he was served with, and he spent the evening in the library of the establishment, pretending to read an article in an American magazine. He failed to discover what it was about; it appeared in a dim way to be about Marian Fancourt.

Quite late in the week she wrote to him that she was not to go into the country—it had only just been settled. Her father, she added, would never settle anything, but put it all on her. She felt her responsibility—she had to— and since she was forced this was the way she had decided. She mentioned no reasons, which gave our friend all the clearer field for bold conjecture about them. In Manchester Square on this second Sunday he esteemed his fortune less good, for she had three or four other visitors. But there were three or four compensations; perhaps the greatest of which was that, learning how her father had after all, at the last hour, gone out of town alone, the bold conjecture I just now spoke of found itself becoming a shade more bold. And then her presence was her presence, and the personal red room was there and was full of it, whatever phantoms passed and vanished, emitting incomprehensible sounds. Lastly, he had the resource of staying till every one had come and gone and of believing this grateful to her, though she gave no particular sign. When they were alone together he came to his point. "But St.

George did come—last Sunday. I saw him as I looked back."

"Yes, but it was the last time."

"The last time?"

"He said he would never come again."

Paul Overt stared. "Does he mean he wishes to cease to see you?"

"I don't know what he means," the girl bravely smiled. "He won't at any rate see me here."

"And pray why not?"

"I haven't the least idea," said Marian Fancourt, whose visitor found her more perversely sublime than ever yet as she professed this clear helplessness.

V

"OH I say, I want you to stop a little," Henry St. George said to him at eleven o'clock the night he dined with the head of the profession. The company—none of it indeed *of* the profession—had been numerous and was taking its leave; our young man, after bidding good-night to his hostess, had put out his hand in farewell to the master of the house. Besides drawing from the latter the protest I have cited this movement provoked a further priceless word about their chance now to have a talk, their going into his room, his having still everything to say. Paul Overt was all delight at this kindness; nevertheless he mentioned in weak jocose qualification the bare fact that he had promised to go to another place which was at a considerable distance.

"Well then you'll break your promise, that's all. You quite awful humbug!" St. George added in a tone that confirmed our young man's ease.

"Certainly I'll break it—but it was a real promise."

"Do you mean to Miss Fancourt? You're following her?" his friend asked.

He answered by a question. "Oh is *she* going?"

"Base imposter!" his ironic host went on. "I've treated you handsomely on the article of that young lady: I won't make another concession. Wait three minutes—I'll be with you." He gave himself to his departing guests, accompanied the long-trained ladies to the door. It was a hot night the windows were open, the sound of the quick carriages and of the linkmen's call came into the house. The affair had rather glittered; a sense of festal things was in the heavy air: not only the influence of that particular entertainment, but the suggestion of the

wide hurry of pleasure which in London on summer nights
fills so many of the happier quarters of the complicated
town. Gradually Mrs. St. George's drawing-room
emptied itself; Paul was left alone with his hostess, to
whom he explained the motive of his waiting. "Ah yes,
some intellectual, some *professional*, talk," she leered; "at
this season doesn't one miss it? Poor dear Henry, I'm so
glad!" The young man looked out of the window a moment, at the called hansoms that lurched up, at the
smooth broughams that rolled away. When he turned
round Mrs. St. George had disappeared; her husband's
voice rose to him from below—he was laughing and talking, in the portico, with some lady who awaited her carriage. Paul had solitary possession, for some minutes, of
the warm deserted rooms where the covered tinted lamplight was soft, the seats had been pushed about and the
odour of flowers lingered. They were large, they were
pretty, they contained objects of value; everything in the
picture told of a "good house." At the end of five minutes
a servant came in with a request from the Master that
he would join him downstairs; upon which, descending,
he followed his conductor through a long passage to an
apartment thrown out, in the rear of the habitation, for
the special requirements, as he guessed, of a busy man of
letters.

St. George was in his shirt-sleeves in the middle of a
large high room—a room without windows, but with a
wide skylight at the top, that of a place of exhibition. It
was furnished as a library, and the serried book-shelves
rose to the ceiling, a surface of incomparable tone produced by dimly-gilt "backs" interrupted here and there
by the suspension of old prints and drawings. At the end
furthest from the door of admission was a tall desk, of
great extent, at which the person using it could write only
in the erect posture of a clerk in a counting-house; and
stretched from the entrance to this structure was a wide
plain band of crimson cloth, as straight as a garden-path

and almost as long, where, in his mind's eye, Paul at once beheld the Master pace to and fro during vexed hours— hours, that is, of admirable composition. The servant gave him a coat, an old jacket with a hang of experience, from a cupboard in the wall, retiring afterwards with the garment he had taken off. Paul Overt welcomed the coat; it was a coat for talk, it promised confidences—having visibly received so many—and had tragic literary elbows. "Ah we're practical—we're practical!" St. George said as he saw his visitor look the place over. "Isn't it a good big cage for going round and round? My wife invented it and she locks me up here every morning."

Our young man breathed—by way of tribute—with a certain oppression. "You don't miss a window—a place to look out?"

"I did at first awfully; but her calculation was just. It saves time, it has saved me many months in these ten years. Here I stand, under the eye of day—in London of course, very often, it's rather a bleared old eye—walled in to my trade. I can't get away—so the room's a fine lesson in concentration. I've learnt the lesson, I think; look at that big bundle of proofs and acknowledge it." He pointed to a fat roll of papers, on one of the tables, which had not been undone.

"Are you bringing out another—?" Paul asked in a tone the fond deficiencies of which he didn't recognise till his companion burst out laughing, and indeed scarce even then.

"You humbug, you humbug!"—St. George appeared to enjoy caressing him, as it were, with that opprobrium. "Don't I know what you think of them?" he asked, standing there with his hands in his pockets and with a new kind of smile. It was as if he were going to let his young votary see him all now."

"Upon my word in that case you know more than I do!" the latter ventured to respond, revealing a part of the torment of being able neither clearly to esteem nor distinctly to renounce him.

"My dear fellow," said the more and more interesting Master, "don't imagine I talk about my books specifically; they're not a decent subject—il ne manquerait plus que ça! I'm not so bad as you may apprehend. About myself, yes, a little, if you like; though it wasn't for that I brought you down here. I want to ask you something—very much indeed; I value this chance. Therefore sit down. We're practical, but there *is* a sofa, you see—for she does humour my poor bones so far. Like all really great administrators and disciplinarians she knows when wisely to relax." Paul sank into the corner of a deep leathern couch, but his friend remained standing and explanatory. "If you don't mind, in this room, this is my habit. From the door to the desk and from the desk to the door. That shakes up my imagination gently; and don't you see what a good thing it is that there's no window for her to fly out of? The eternal standing as I write (I stop at that bureau and put it down, when anything comes, and so we go on) was rather wearisome at first, but we adopted it with an eye to the long run: you're in better order—if your legs don't break down!—and you can keep it up for more years. Oh we're practical—we're practical!" St. George repeated, going to the table and taking up all mechanically the bundle of proofs. But, pulling off the wrapper, he had a change of attention that appealed afresh to our hero. He lost himself a moment, examining the sheets of his new book, while the younger man's eyes wandered over the room again.

"Lord, what good things I should do if I had such a charming place as this to do them in!" Paul reflected. The outer world, the world of accident and ugliness, was so successfully excluded, and within the rich protecting square, beneath the patronising sky, the dream-figures, the summoned company, could hold their particular revel. It was a fond prevision of Overt's rather than an observation on actual data, for which occasions had been too few, that the Master thus more closely viewed would have the quality, the charming gift, of flashing out, all surprisingly, in personal intercourse and at moments of suspended or perhaps even of diminished expectation. A happy relation with him would be a thing proceeding by jumps, not by traceable stages.

"Do you read them—really?" he asked, laying down the proofs on Paul's enquiring of him how soon the work would be published. And when the young man answered "Oh yes, always," he was moved to mirth again by something he caught in his manner of saying that. "You go to see your grandmother on her birthday—and very proper it is, especially as she won't last for ever. She has lost every faculty and every sense; she neither sees, nor hears, nor speaks; but all customary pieties and kindly habits are respectable. Only you're strong if you *do* read 'em! *I* couldn't, my dear fellow. You *are* strong, I know; and that's just a part of what I wanted to say to you. You're very strong indeed. I've been going into your other things —they've interested me immensely. Some one ought to have told me about them before—some one I could believe. But whom can one believe? You're wonderfully on the right road—it's awfully decent work. Now do you mean to keep it up?—that's what I want to ask you."

"Do I mean to do others?" Paul asked, looking up from his sofa at his erect inquisitor and feeling partly like a happy little boy when the schoolmaster is gay, and partly like some pilgrim of old who might have consulted a world-famous oracle. St. George's own performance had been infirm, but as an adviser he would be infallible.

"Others—others? Ah the number won't matter; one other would do, if it were really a further step—a throb of the same effort. What I mean is have you it in your heart to go in for some sort of decent perfection?"

"Ah decency, ah perfection—!" the young man sincerely sighed. "I talked of them the other Sunday with Miss Fancourt."

It produced on the Master's part a laugh of odd acrimony. "Yes, they'll 'talk' of them as much as you like! But they'll do little to help one to them. There's no obligation of course; only you strike me as capable," he went on. "You must have thought it all over. I can't believe you're without a plan. That's the sensation you give me, and it's so rare that it really stirs one up—it makes you remarkable. If you haven't a plan, if you *don't* mean to keep it up, surely you're within your rights; it's nobody's business, no one can force you, and not more than two or three people will notice you don't go straight. The others—*all* the rest, every blest soul in England, will think you do—will think you *are* keeping it up: upon my honour they will! I shall be one of the two or three who know better. Now the question is whether you can do it for two or three. Is that the stuff you're made of?"

It locked his guest a minute as in closed throbbing arms. "I could do it for one, if you were the one."

"Don't say that; I don't deserve it; it scorches me," he protested with eyes suddenly grave and glowing. "The 'one' is of course one's self, one's conscience, one's idea, the singleness of one's aim. I think of that pure spirit as a man thinks of a woman he has in some detested hour of his youth loved and forsaken. She haunts him with reproachful eyes, she lives for ever before him. As an artist, you know, I've married for money." Paul stared and even blushed a little, confounded by this avowal; whereupon his host, observing the expression of his face, dropped a quick laugh and pursued: "You don't follow my figure. I'm not speaking of my dear wife, who had a small fortune—which, however, was not my bribe. I fell in love with her, as many other people have done. I refer to the mercenary muse whom I led to the altar of literature. Don't, my boy, put your nose into *that* yoke. The awful jade will lead you a life!"

Our hero watched him, wondering and deeply touched. "Haven't you been happy!"

"Happy? It's a kind of hell."

"There are things I should like to ask you," Paul said after a pause.

"Ask me anything in all the world. I'd turn myself inside out to save you."

"To 'save' me?" he quavered.

"To make you stick to it—to make you see it through. As I said to you the other night at Summersoft, let my example be vivid to you."

"Why your books are not so bad as that," said Paul, fairly laughing and feeling that if ever a fellow had breathed the air of art—!

"So bad as what?"

"Your talent's so great that it's in everything you do, in what's less good as well as in what's best. You've some forty volumes to show for it—forty volumes of wonderful life, of rare observation, of magnificent ability."

"I'm very clever, of course I know that"—but it was a thing, in fine, this author made nothing of. "Lord, what rot they'd all be if I hadn't been! I'm a successful charlatan," he went on—"I've been able to pass off my system. But do you know what it is? It's *carton-pierre*."

"*Carton-pierre?*" Paul was struck, and gaped.

"Lincrusta-Walton!"

"Ah don't say such things—you make me bleed!" the younger man protested. "I see you in a beautiful fortunate home, living in comfort and honour."

"Do you call it honour?"—his host took him up with an intonation that often comes back to him. "That's what I want *you* to go in for. I mean the real thing. This is brummagem."

"Brummagem?" Paul ejaculated while his eyes wandered, by a movement natural at the moment, over the luxurious room.

"Ah they make it so well to-day—it's wonderfully deceptive!"

Our friend thrilled with the interest and perhaps even more with the pity of it. Yet he wasn't afraid to seem to patronise when he could still so far envy. "Is it deceptive that I find you living with every appearance of domestic felicity—blest with a devoted, accomplished wife, with children whose acquaintance I haven't yet had the pleasure of making, but who *must* be delightful young people, from what I know of their parents?"

St. George smiled as for the candour of his question. "It's all excellent, my dear fellow—heaven forbid I should deny it. I've made a great deal of money; my wife has known how to take care of it, to use it without wasting it, to put a good bit of it by, to make it fructify. I've got a loaf on the shelf; I've got everything in fact but the great thing."

"The great thing?" Paul kept echoing.

"The sense of having done the best—the sense which is the real life of the artist and the absence of which is his death, of having drawn from his intellectual instrument the finest music that nature had hidden in it, of having played it as it should be played. He either does that or he doesn't—and if he doesn't he isn't worth speaking of. Therefore, precisely, those who really know *don't* speak of him. He may still hear a great chatter, but what he hears most is the incorruptible silence of Fame. I've squared her, you may say, for my little hour—but what's my little hour? Don't imagine for a moment," the Master pursued, "that I'm such a cad as to have brought you down here to abuse or to complain of my wife to you. She's a woman of distinguished qualities, to whom my obligations are immense; so that, if you please, we'll say nothing about her. My boys—my children are all boys—are straight and strong, thank God, and have no poverty of growth about them, no penury of needs. I receive periodically the most satisfactory attestation from Harrow, from Oxford, from Sandhurst—oh we've done the best for them!—of their eminence as living thriving consuming organisms."

"It must be delightful to feel that the son of one's loins is at Sandhurst," Paul remarked enthusiastically.

"It is—it's charming. Oh I'm a patriot!"

The young man then could but have the greater tribute of questions to pay. "Then what did you mean—the other night at Summersoft—by saying that children are a curse?"

"My dear youth, on what basis are we talking?" and St. George dropped upon the sofa at a short distance from him. Sitting a little sideways he leaned back against the opposite arm with his hands raised and interlocked behind his head. "On the supposition that a certain perfection's possible and even desirable—isn't it so? Well, all I say is that one's children interfere with perfection. One's wife interferes. Marriage interferes."

"You think then the artist shouldn't marry?"

"He does so at his peril—he does so at his cost."

"Not even when his wife's in sympathy with his work?"

"She never is—she can't be! Women haven't a conception of such things."

"Surely they on occasion work themselves," Paul objected.

"Yes, very badly indeed. Oh of course, often, they think they understand, they think they sympathise. Then it is they're most dangerous. Their idea is that you shall do a great lot and get a great lot of money. Their great nobleness and virtue, their exemplary conscientiousness as British females, is in keeping you up to that. My wife makes all my bargains with my publishers for me, and has done so for twenty years. She does it consummately well—that's why I'm really pretty well off. Aren't you the father of their innocent babes, and will you withhold from them their natural sustenance? You asked me the other night if they're not an immense incentive. Of course they are—there's no doubt of that!"

Paul turned it over: it took, from eyes he had never felt open so wide, so much looking at. "For myself I've an idea I need incentives."

"Ah well then, n'en parlons plus!" his companion handsomely smiled.

"*You* are an incentive, I maintain," the young man went on. "You don't affect me in the way you'd apparently like to. Your great success is what I see—the pomp of Ennismore Gardens!"

"Success?"—St. George's eyes had a cold fine light. "Do you call it success to be spoken of as you'd speak of me if you were sitting here with another artist—a young man intelligent and sincere like yourself? Do you call it success to make you blush—as you *would* blush! —if some foreign critic (some fellow, of course I mean, who should know what he was talking about and should have shown you he did, as foreign critics like to show it) were to say to you: 'He's the one, in this country, whom they consider the most perfect, isn't he?' Is it success to be the occasion of a young Englishman's having to stammer as you would have to stammer at such a moment for old England? No, no; success is to have made people wriggle to another tune. Do try it!"

Paul continued all gravely to glow. "Try what?"

"Try to do some really good work."

"Oh I want to, heaven knows!"

"Well, you can't do it without sacrifices—don't believe that for a moment," the Master said. "I've made none. I've had everything. In other words I've missed everything."

"You've had the full rich masculine human general life, with all the responsibilities and duties and burdens and sorrows and joys—all the domestic and social initiations and complications. They must be immensely suggestive, immensely amusing," Paul anxiously submitted.

"Amusing?"

"For a strong man—yes."

"They've given me subjects without number, if that's what you mean; but they've taken away at the same time the power to use them. I've touched a thousand things, but which one of them have I turned into gold? The artist has to do only with that—he knows nothing of any baser metal. I've led the life of the world, with my wife and my progeny; the clumsy conventional expensive materialised vulgarised brutalised life of London. We've got everything handsome, even a carriage—we're perfect Philistines and prosperous hospitable eminent people. But, my dear fellow, don't try to stultify yourself and pretend you don't know what we *haven't* got. It's bigger than all the rest. Between artists—come!" the Master wound up. "You know as well as you sit there that you'd put a pistol-ball into your brain if you had written my books!"

It struck his listener that the tremendous talk promised by him at Summersoft had indeed come off, and with a promptitude, a fulness, with which the latter's young imagination had scarcely reckoned. His impression fairly shook him and he throbbed with the excitement of such deep soundings and such strange confidences. He throbbed indeed with the conflict of his feelings—bewilderment and recognition and alarm, enjoyment and protest and assent, all commingled with tenderness (and a kind of shame in the participation) for the sores and bruises exhibited by so fine a creature, and with a sense of the tragic secret nursed under his trappings. The idea of *his*, Paul Overt's, becoming the occasion of such an act of humility made him flush and pant, at the same time that his consciousness was in certain directions too much alive not to swallow—and not intensely to taste—every offered spoonful of the revelation. It had been his odd fortune to blow upon the deep waters, to make them surge and break in waves of strange eloquence. But how couldn't he give out a passionate contradiction of his host's last extravagance, how couldn't he enumerate to him the parts of his work he loved, the splendid things he had found in it, beyond the compass of any other writer of the day? St. George listened a while, courteously; then he said, laying his hand on his visitor's: "That's all very well; and if your idea's to do nothing better there's no reason you shouldn't have as many good things as I—as many human and material appendages, as many sons or daughters, a wife with as many gowns, a house with as many servants, a stable with as many horses, a heart with as many aches." The Master got up when he had spoken thus—he stood a moment—near the sofa looking down on his agitated pupil. "Are you possessed of any property?" it occurred to him to ask.

"None to speak of."

"Oh well then there's no reason why you shouldn't make a goodish income—if you set about it the right way. Study *me* for that—study me well. You may really have horses."

Paul sat there some minutes without speaking. He looked straight before him—he turned over many things. His friend had wandered away, taking up a parcel of letters from the table where the roll of proofs had lain. "What was the book Mrs. St. George made you burn—the one she didn't like?" our young man brought out.

"The book she made me burn—how did you know that?" The Master looked up from his letters quite without the facial convulsion the pupil had feared.

"I heard her speak of it at Summersoft."

"Ah yes—she's proud of it. I don't know—it was rather good."

"What was it about?"

"Let me see." And he seemed to make an effort to remember. "Oh yes—it was about myself." Paul gave an irrepressible groan for the disappearance of such a production, and the elder man went on: "Oh but *you* should write it—*you* should do me." And he pulled up—from the restless motion that had come upon him; his fine smile a generous glare. "There's a subject, my boy: no end of stuff in it!"

Again Paul was silent, but it was all tormenting. "Are there no women who really understand—who can take part in a sacrifice?"

"How can they take part? They themselves are the sacrifice. They're the idol and the altar and the flame."

"Isn't there even *one* who sees further?" Paul continued.

For a moment St. George made no answer; after which, having torn up his letters, he came back to the point all ironic. "Of course I know the one you mean. But not even Miss Fancourt."

"I thought you admired her so much."

"It's impossible to admire her more. **Are you in love** with her?" St. George asked.

"Yes," Paul Overt presently said.

"Well then give it up."

Paul stared. "Give up my 'love'?"

"Bless me, no. Your idea." And then as our hero but still gazed: "The one you talked with her about. The idea of a decent perfection."

"She'd help it—she'd help it!" the young man cried.

"For about a year—the first year, yes. After that she'd be as a millstone round its neck."

Paul frankly wondered. "Why she has a passion for the real thing, for good work—for everything you and I care for most."

"'You and I' is charming, my dear fellow!" his friend laughed. "She has it indeed, but she'd have a still greater passion for her children—and very proper too. She'd insist on everything's being made comfortable, advantageous, propitious for them. That isn't the artist's business."

"The artist—the artist! Isn't he a man all the same?"

St. George had a grand grimace. "I mostly think not. You know as well as I what he has to do: the concentration, the finish, the independence he must strive for from the moment he begins to wish his work really decent. Ah my young friend, his relation to women, and especially to the one he's most intimately concerned with, is at the mercy of the damning fact that whereas he can in the nature of things have but one standard, they have about fifty. That's what makes them so superior," St. George amusingly added. "Fancy an artist with a change of standards as you'd have a change of shirts or of dinner-plates. To *do* it—to do it and make it divine—is the only thing he has to think about. 'Is it done or not?' is his only question. Not 'Is it done as well as a proper solicitude for my dear little family will allow?' He has nothing to do with the relative—he has only to do with the absolute; and a dear little family may represent a dozen relatives."

"Then you don't allow him the common passions and affections ot men?" Paul asked.

"Hasn't he a passion, an affection, which includes all the rest? Besides, let him have all the passions he likes—if he only keeps his independence. He must be able to be poor."

Paul slowly got up. "Why then did you advise me to make up to her?"

St. George laid a hand on his shoulder. "Because she'd make a splendid wife! And I hadn't read you then."

The young man had a strained smile. "I wish you had left me alone!"

"I didn't know that that wasn't good enough for you," his host returned.

"What a false position, what a condemnation of the artist, that he's a mere disfranchised monk and can produce his effect only by giving up personal happiness. What an arraignment of art!" Paul went on with a trembling voice.

"Ah you don't imagine by chance that I'm defending art? 'Arraignment'—I should think so! Happy the societies in which it hasn't made its appearance, for from the moment it comes they have a consuming ache, they have an incurable corruption, in their breast. Most assuredly is the artist in a false position! But I thought we were taking him for granted. Pardon me," St. George continued: "'Ginistrella' made me!"

Paul stood looking at the floor—one o'clock struck, in the stillness, from a neighbouring church-tower. "Do you think she'd ever look at me?" he put to his friend at last.

"Miss Fancourt—as a suitor? Why shouldn't I think it? That's why I've tried to favour you—I've had a little chance or two of bettering your opportunity."

"Forgive my asking you, but do you mean by keeping away yourself?" Paul said with a blush.

"I'm an old idiot—my place isn't there," St. George stated gravely.

"I'm nothing yet, I've no fortune; and there must be so many others," his companion pursued.

The Master took this considerably in, but made little of it. "You're a gentleman and a man of genius. I think you might do something."

"But if I must give that up—the genius?"

"Lots of people, you know, think I've kept mine," St. George wonderfully grinned.

"You've a genius for mystification!" Paul declared, but grasping his hand gratefully in attenuation of this judgement.

"Poor dear boy, I do worry you! But try, try, all the same. I think your chances are good and you'll win a great prize."

Paul held fast the other's hand a minute; he looked into the strange deep face. "No, I *am* an artist—I can't help it!"

"Ah show it then!" St. George pleadingly broke out. "Let me see before I die the thing I most want, the thing I yearn for: a life in which the passion—ours—is really intense. If you can be rare don't fail of it! Think what it is—how it counts—how it lives!"

They had moved to the door and he had closed both his hands over his companion's. Here they paused again and our hero breathed deep. "I want to live!"

"In what sense?"

"In the greatest."

"Well then stick to it—see it through."

"With your sympathy—your help?"

"Count on that—you'll be a great figure to me. Count on my highest appreciation, my devotion. You'll give me satisfaction—if that has any weight with you!" After which, as Paul appeared still to waver, his host added: "Do you remember what you said to me at Summersoft?"

"Something infatuated, no doubt!"

" 'I'll do anything in the world you tell me.' You said that."

"And you hold me to it?"

"Ah what am I?" the Master expressively sighed.

"Lord, what things I shall have to do!" Paul almost moaned as he departed.

VI

"It goes on too much abroad—hang abroad!" These or something like them had been the Master's remarkable words in relation to the action of "Ginistrella"; and yet, though they had made a sharp impression on the author of that work, like almost all spoken words from the same source, he a week after the conversation I have noted left England for a long absence and full of brave intentions. It is not a perversion of the truth to pronounce that encounter the direct cause of his departure. If the oral utterance of the eminent writer had the privilege of moving him deeply it was especially on his turning it over at leisure, hours and days later, that it appeared to yield him its full meaning and exhibit its extreme importance. He spent the summer in Switzerland and, having in September begun a new task, determined not to cross the Alps till he should have made a good start. To this end he returned to a quiet corner he knew well, on the edge of the Lake of Geneva and within sight of the towers of Chillon: a region and a view for which he had an affection that sprang from old associations and was capable of mysterious revivals and refreshments. Here he lingered late, till the snow was on the nearer hills, almost down to the limit to which he could climb when his stint, on the shortening afternoons, was performed. The autumn was fine, the lake was blue and his book took form and direction. These felicities, for the time, embroidered his life, which he suffered to cover him with its mantle. At the end of six weeks he felt he had learnt St. George's lesson by heart, had tested and proved its doctrine. Nevertheless he did a very inconsistent thing: before crossing the Alps he wrote to Marian Fancourt. He was aware of the perversity of this act, and it was only as a luxury, an amusement, the reward of a strenuous autumn, that he justified it. She had asked of him no such favour when, shortly before he left London, three days after their dinner in Ennismore Gardens, he went to take leave of her. It was true she had had no ground—he hadn't named his intention of absence. He had kept his counsel for want of due assurance: it was that particular visit that was, the next thing, to settle the matter. He had paid the visit to see how much he really cared for her, and quick departure, without so much as an explicit farewell, was the sequel to this enquiry, the answer to which had created within him a deep yearning. When he wrote her from Clarens he noted that he owed her an explanation (more than three months after!) for not having told her what he was doing.

She replied now briefly but promptly, and gave him a striking piece of news; that of the death, a week before, of Mrs. St. George. This exemplary woman had succumbed, in the country, to a violent attack of inflammation of the lungs—he would remember that for a long time she had been delicate. Miss Fancourt added that she believed her husband overwhelmed by the blow; he would miss her too terribly—she had been everything in life to him. Paul Overt, on this, immediately wrote to St. George. He would from the day of their parting have been glad to remain in communication with him, but had hitherto lacked the right excuse for troubling so busy a man. Their long nocturnal talk came back to him in every detail, but this was no bar to an expression of proper sympathy with the head of the profession, for hadn't that very talk made it clear that the late accomplished lady was the influence that ruled his life? What catastrophe could be more cruel than the extinction of such an influence? This was to be exactly the tone taken by St. George in answering his young friend upwards of a month later. He made no allusion of course to their important discussion. He spoke of his wife as frankly and generously as if he had quite forgotten that occasion, and the feeling of deep bereavement was visible in his words. "Sh. took everything off my hands—off my mind. She car.ed on our life with the greatest art, the rarest devot'un, and I was free, as few men can have been, to drive .uy pen, to shut myself up with my trade. This was a rare service—the highest she could have rendered me. Would I could have acknowledged it more fitly!"

A certain bewilderment, for our hero, disengaged itself from these remarks: they struck him as a contradiction, a retractation, strange on the part of a man who hadn't the excuse of witlessness. He had certainly not expected his correspondent to rejoice in the death of his wife, and it was perfectly in order that the rupture of a tie of more than twenty years should have left him sore. But if she had been so clear a blessing what in the name of consistency had the dear man meant by turning *him* upside down that night —by dosing him to that degree, at the most sensitive hour of his life, with the doctrine of renunciation? If Mrs. St. George was an irreparable loss, then her husband's inspired advice had been a bad joke and renunciation was a mistake. Overt was on the point of rushing back to London to show that, for his part, he was perfectly willing to consider it so, and he went so far as to take the manuscript of the first chapters of his new book out of his table-drawer and insert it into a pocket of his portmanteau. This led to his catching a glimpse of certain pages he hadn't looked at for months, and that accident, in turn, to his being struck with the high promise they revealed—a rare result of such retrospections, which it was his habit to avoid as much as possible: they usually brought home to him that the glow of composition might be a purely subjective and misleading emotion. On this occasion a certain belief in himself disengaged itself whimsically from the serried erasures of his first draft, making him think it best after all to pursue his present trial to the end. If he could write so well under the rigour of privation it might be a mistake to change the conditions before that spell had spent itself. He would go back to London of course, but he would go back only when he should have finished his book. This was the vow he privately made, restoring his manuscript to the table-drawer. It may be added that it took him a long time to finish his book, for the subject was as difficult as it was fine, and he was literally embarrassed by the fulness of his notes. Something within him warned him he must make it supremely good—otherwise he should lack, as regards his private behaviour, a handsome excuse. He had a horror of this deficiency and found himself as firm as need be on the question of the lamp and the file. He crossed the Alps at last and spent the winter, the spring, the ensuing summer, in Italy, where still, at the end of a twelvemonth, his task was unachieved. "Stick to it—see it through": this general injunction of St. George's was good also for the particular case. He applied it to the utmost, with the result that when in its slow order the summer had come round again he felt he had given all that was in him. This time he put his papers into his pormanteau, with the address of his publisher attached, and took his way northward.

He had been absent from London for two years; two years which, seeming to count as more, had made such a difference in his own life—through the production of a novel far stronger, he believed, than "Ginistrella"—that he turned out into Piccadilly, the morning after his arrival, with a vague expectation of changes, of finding great things had happened. But there were few transformations in Piccadilly—only three or four big red houses where there had been low black ones—and the brightness of the end of June peeped through the rusty railings of the Green Park and glittered in the varnish of the rolling carriages as he had seen it in other, more cursory Junes. It was a greeting he appreciated; it seemed friendly and pointed, added to the exhilaration of his finished book, of his having his own country and the huge oppressive amusing city that suggested everything, that contained everything, under his hand again. "Stay at home and do things here—do sub-

jects we can measure," St. George had said; and now it
struck him he should ask nothing better than to stay at
home for ever. Late in the afternoon he took his way to
Manchester Square, looking out for a number he hadn't
forgotten. Miss Fancourt, however, was not at home, so
that he turned rather dejectedly from the door. His movement brought him face to face with a gentleman just ap-
proaching it and recognised on another glance as Miss
Fancourt's father. Paul saluted this personage, and the
General returned the greeting with his customary good
manner—a manner so good, however, that you could never
tell whether it meant he placed you. The disappointed
caller felt the impulse to address him; then, hesitating,
became both aware of having no particular remark to
make, and convinced that though the old soldier remembered him he remembered him wrong. He therefore went
his way without computing the irresistible effect his own
evident recognition would have on the General, who never
neglected a chance to gossip. Our young man's face was
expressive, and observation seldom let it pass. He hadn't
taken ten steps before he heard himself called after with
a friendly semi-articulate "Er—I beg your pardon!" He
turned round and the General, smiling at him from the
porch, said: "Won't you come in? I won't leave you the
advantage of me!" Paul declined to come in, and then
felt regret, for Miss Fancourt, so late in the afternoon,
might return at any moment. But her father gave him
no second chance; he appeared mainly to wish not to have
struck him as ungracious. A further look at the visitor
had recalled something, enough at least to enable him
to say: "You've come back, you've come back?" Paul was
on the point of replying that he had come back the night
before, but he suppressed, the next instant, this strong
light on the immediacy of his visit and, giving merely a
general assent, alluded to the young lady he deplored not
having found. He had come late in the hope she would be
in. "I'll tell her—I'll tell her," said the old man; and then

he added quickly, gallantly: "You'll be giving us something new? It's a long time, isn't it?" Now he remembered him right.

"Rather long. I'm very slow," Paul explained. "I met you at Summersoft a long time ago."

"Oh yes—with Henry St. George. I remember very well. Before his poor wife—" General Fancourt paused a moment, smiling a little less. "I dare say you know."

"About Mrs. St. George's death? Certainly—I heard at the time."

"Oh no, I mean—I mean he's to be married."

"Ah I've not heard that!" But just as Paul was about to add "To whom?" the General crossed his intention.

"When did you come back? I know you've been away— by my daughter. She was very sorry. You ought to give her something new."

"I came back last night," said our young man, to whom something had occurred which made his speech for the moment a little thick.

"Ah most kind of you to come so soon. Couldn't you turn up at dinner?"

"At dinner?" Paul just mechanically repeated, not liking to ask whom St. George was going to marry, but thinking only of that.

"There are several people, I believe. Certainly St. George. Or afterwards if you like better. I believe my daughter expects—" He appeared to notice something in the visitor's raised face (on his steps he stood higher) which led him to interrupt himself, and the interruption gave him a momentary sense of awkwardness, from which he sought a quick issue. "Perhaps then you haven't heard she's to be married."

Paul gaped again. "To be married?"

"To Mr. St. George—it has just been settled. Odd marriage, isn't it?" Our listener uttered no opinion on this point: he only continued to stare. "But I dare say it will do—she's so awfully literary!" said the General.

Paul had turned very red. "Oh it's a surprise—very interesting, very charming! I'm afraid I can't dine—so many thanks!"

"Well, you must come to the wedding!" cried the General. "Oh I remember that day at Summersoft. He's a great man, you know."

"Charming—charming!" Paul stammered for retreat. He shook hands with the General and got off. His face was red and he had the sense of its growing more and more crimson. All the evening at home—he went straight to his rooms and remained there dinnerless—his cheek burned at intervals as if it had been smitten. He didn't understand what had happened to him, what trick had been played him, what treachery practised. "None, none," he said to himself. "I've nothing to do with it. I'm out of it—it's none of my business." But that bewildered murmur was followed again and again by the incongruous ejaculation: "Was it a plan—was it a plan?" Sometimes he cried to himself, breathless, "Have I been duped, sold, swindled?" If at all, he was an absurd, an abject victim. It was as if he hadn't lost her till now. He had renounced her, yes; but that was another affair—that was a closed but not a locked door. Now he seemed to see the door quite slammed in his face. Did he expect her to wait—was she to give him his time like that: two years at a stretch? He didn't know what he had expected—he only knew what he hadn't. It wasn't this—it wasn't this. Mystification bitterness and wrath rose and boiled in him when he thought of the deference, the devotion, the credulity with which he had listened to St. George. The evening wore on and the light was long; but even when it had darkened he remained without a lamp. He had flung himself on the sofa, where he lay through the hours with his eyes either closed or gazing at the gloom, in the attitude of a man teaching himself to bear something, to bear having been made a fool of. He had made it too easy—that idea passed over him like a hot wave. Suddenly, as he heard eleven o'clock strike, he

jumped up, remembering what General Fancourt had said
about his coming after dinner. He'd go—he'd see her at
least; perhaps he should see what it meant. He felt as if
some of the elements of a hard sum had been given him
and the others were wanting: he couldn't do his sum till
he had got all his figures.

He dressed and drove quickly, so that by half-past
eleven he was at Manchester Square. There were a good
many carriages at the door—a party was going on; a circumstance which at the last gave him a slight relief, for
now he would rather see her in a crowd. People passed him
on the staircase; they were going away, going "on" with
the hunted herdlike movement of London society at night.
But sundry groups remained in the drawing-room, and it
was some minutes, as she didn't hear him announced, before he discovered and spoke to her. In this short interval
he had seen St. George talking to a lady before the fire-
place; but he at once looked away, feeling unready for an
encounter, and therefore couldn't be sure the author of
"Shadowmere" noticed him. At all events he didn't come
over; though Miss Fancourt did as soon as she saw him—
she almost rushed at him, smiling rustling radiant beautiful. He had forgotten what her head, what her face offered
to the sight; she was in white, there were gold figures on
her dress and her hair was a casque of gold. He saw in
a single moment that she was happy, happy with an aggres-
sive splendour. But she wouldn't speak to him of that, she
would speak only of himself.

"I'm so delighted; my father told me. How kind of you
to come!" She struck him as so fresh and brave, while his
eyes moved over her, that he said to himself irresistibly:
"Why to *him*, why not to youth, to strength, to ambition,
to a future? Why, in her rich young force, to failure, to
abdication, to superannuation?" In his thought at that
sharp moment he blasphemed even against all that had
been left of his faith in the peccable master. "I'm so sorry

I missed you," she went on. "My father told me. How charming of you to have come so soon!"

"Does that surprise you?" Paul Overt asked.

"The first day? No, from you—nothing that's nice." She was interrupted by a lady who bade her good-night, and he seemed to read that it cost her nothing to speak to him in that tone; it was her old liberal lavish way, with a certain added amplitude that time had brought; and if this manner began to operate on the spot, at such a juncture in her history, perhaps in the other days too it had meant just as little or as much—a mere mechanical charity, with the difference now that she was satisfied, ready to give but in want of nothing. Oh she was satisfied—and why shouldn't she be? Why shouldn't she have been surprised at his coming the first day—for all the good she had ever got from him? As the lady continued to hold her attention Paul turned from her with a strange irritation in his complicated artistic soul and a sort of disinterested disappointment. She was so happy that it was almost stupid—a disproof of the extraordinary intelligence he had formerly found in her. Didn't she know how bad St. George could be, hadn't she recognised the awful thinness—? If she didn't she was nothing, and if she did why such an insolence of serenity? This question expired as our young man's eyes settled at last on the genius who had advised him in a great crisis. St. George was still before the chimney-piece, but now he was alone—fixed, waiting, as if he meant to stop after every one—and he met the clouded gaze of the young friend so troubled as to the degree of his right (the right his resentment would have enjoyed) to regard himself as a victim. Somehow the ravage of the question was checked by the Master's radiance. It was as fine in its way as Marian Fancourt's, it denoted the happy human being; but also it represented to Paul Overt that the author of "Shadowmere" had now definitely ceased to count—ceased to count as a writer. As he smiled a welcome across the place he was almost *banal*, was almost smug. Paul fancied that for a moment he hesitated to make a movement, as if, for all the world, he *had* his bad conscience; then they had already met in the middle of the room and had shaken hands—expressively, cordially on St. George's part. With which they had passed back together to where the elder man had been standing, while St. George said: "I hope you're never going away again. I've been dining here; the General told me." He was handsome, he was young, he looked as if he had still a great fund of life. He bent the friendliest, most unconfessing eyes on his disciple of a couple of years before; asked him about everything, his health, his plans, his late occupations, the new book. "When will it be out—soon, soon, I hope? Splendid, eh? That's right; you're a comfort, you're a luxury! I've read you all over again these last six months." Paul waited to see if he'd tell him what the General had told him in the afternoon and what Miss Fancourt, verbally at least, of course hadn't. But as it didn't come out he at last put the question "Is it true, the great news I hear—that you're to be married?"

"Ah you *have* heard it then?"

"Didn't the General tell you?" Paul asked.

The Master's face was wonderful. "Tell me what?"

"That he mentioned it to me this afternoon?"

"My dear fellow, I don't remember. We've been in the midst of people. I'm sorry, in that case, that I lose the pleasure, myself, of announcing to you a fact that touches me so nearly. It *is* a fact, strange as it may appear. It has only just become one. Isn't it ridiculous?" St. George made this speech without confusion, but on the other hand, so far as our friend could judge, without latent impudence. It struck his interlocutor that, to talk so comfortably and coolly, he must simply have forgotten what had passed between them. His next words, however, showed he hadn't, and they produced, as an appeal to Paul's own memory, an effect which would have been ludicrous if it hadn't been cruel. "Do you recall the talk we had at my house that night, into which Miss Fancourt's name entered? I've often thought of it since."

"Yes; no wonder you said what you did"—Paul was careful to meet his eyes.

"In the light of the present occasion? Ah but there was no light then. How could I have foreseen this hour?"

"Didn't you think it probable?"

"Upon my honour, no," said Henry St. George. "Certainly I owe you that assurance. Think how my situation has changed."

"I see—I see," our young man murmured.

His companion went on as if, now that the subject had been broached, he was, as a person of imagination and tact, quite ready to give every satisfaction—being both by his genius and his method so able to enter into everything another might feel. "But it's not only that; for honestly, at my age, I never dreamed—a widower with big boys and with so little else! It has turned out differently from anything one could have dreamed, and I'm fortunate beyond all measure. She has been so free, and yet she consents. Better than any one else perhaps—for I remember how you liked her before you went away, and how she liked you—you can intelligently congratulate me."

"She has been so free!" Those words made a great impression on Paul Overt, and he almost writhed under that irony in them as to which it so little mattered whether it was designed or casual. Of course she had been free, and appreciably perhaps by his own act; for wasn't the Master's allusion to her having liked him a part of the irony too? "I thought that by your theory you disapproved of a writer's marrying."

"Surely—surely. But you don't call me a writer?"

"You ought to be ashamed," said Paul.

"Ashamed of marrying again?"

"I won't say that—but ashamed of your reasons."

The elder man beautifully smiled. "You must let me judge of them, my good friend."

"Yes; why not? For you judged wonderfully of mine."

The tone of these words appeared suddenly, for St. George, to suggest the unsuspected. He stared as if divining a bitterness. "Don't you think I've been straight?"

"You might have told me at the time perhaps."

"My dear fellow, when I say I couldn't pierce futurity—!"

"I mean afterwards."

The Master wondered. "After my wife's death?"

"When this idea came to you."

"Ah never, never! I wanted to save you, rare and precious as you are."

Poor Overt looked hard at him. "Are you marrying Miss Fancourt to save me?"

"Not absolutely, but it adds to the pleasure. I shall be the making of you," St. George smiled. "I was greatly struck, after our talk, with the brave devoted way you quitted the country, and still more perhaps with your force of character in remaining abroad. You're very strong —you're wonderfully strong."

Paul tried to sound his shining eyes; the strange thing was that he seemed sincere—not a mocking fiend. He turned away, and as he did so heard the Master say something about his giving them all the proof, being the joy of his old age. He faced him again, taking another look. "Do you mean to say you've stopped writing?"

"My dear fellow, of course I have. It's too late. Didn't I tell you?"

"I can't believe it!"

"Of course you can't—with your own talent! No, no; for the rest of my life I shall only read *you*."

"Does she know that—Miss Fancourt?"

"She will—she will." Did he mean this, our young man wondered, as a covert intimation that the assistance he should derive from that young lady's fortune, moderate as it was, would make the difference of putting it in his power to cease to work ungratefully an exhausted vein?

Somehow, standing there in the ripeness of his successful manhood, he didn't suggest that any of his veins were exhausted. "Don't you remember the moral I offered myself to you that night as pointing?" St George continued. "Consider at any rate the warning I am at present."

This was too much—he *was* the mocking fiend. Paul turned from him with a mere nod for good-night and the sense in a sore heart that he might come back to him and his easy grace, his fine way of arranging things, some time in the far future, but couldn't fraternise with him now. It was necessary to his soreness to believe for the hour in the intensity of his grievance—all the more cruel for its not being a legal one. It was doubtless in the attitude of hugging this wrong that he descended the stairs without taking leave of Miss Fancourt, who hadn't been in view at the moment he quitted the room. He was glad to get out into the honest dusky unsophisticating night, to move fast, to take his way home on foot. He walked a long time, going astray, paying no attention. He was thinking of too many other things. His steps recovered their direction, however, and at the end of an hour he found himself before his door in the small inexpensive empty street. He lingered, questioning himself still before going in, with nothing around and above him but moonless blackness, a bad lamp or two and a few far-away dim stars. To these last faint features he raised his eyes; he had been saying to himself that he should have been "sold" indeed, diabolically sold, if now, on his new foundation, at the end of a year, St. George were to put forth something of his prime quality —something of the type of "Shadowmere" and finer than his finest. Greatly as he admired his talent Paul literally hoped such an incident wouldn't occur; it seemed to him just then that he shouldn't be able to bear it. His late adviser's words were still in his ears—"You're very strong, wonderfully strong." Was he really? Certainly he would have to be, and it might a little serve for revenge. *Is* he? the reader may ask in turn, if his interest has followed

the perplexed young man so far. The best answer to that
perhaps is that he's doing his best, but that it's too soon
to say. When the new book came out in the autumn Mr.
and Mrs. St. George found it really magnificent. The
former still has published nothing, but Paul doesn't even
yet feel safe. I may say for him, however, that if this event
were to occur he would really be the very first to appreciate
it: which is perhaps a proof that the Master was essentially right and that Nature had dedicated him to intellectual, not to personal passion.